THE TRESPASSERS

Center Point
Large Print

**This Large Print Book carries the
Seal of Approval of N.A.V.H.**

THE TRESPASSERS

Giles Lutz

CENTER POINT PUBLISHING
THORNDIKE, MAINE

This Center Point Large Print edition
is published in the year 2007 by arrangement with
Golden West Literary Agency.

Copyright © 1965 by Giles A. Lutz.

All rights reserved.

The text of this Large Print edition is unabridged. In other
aspects, this book may vary from the original edition.
Printed in the United States of America.
Set in 16-point Times New Roman type.

ISBN-10: 1-60285-068-2
ISBN-13: 978-1-60285-068-2

Library of Congress Cataloging-in-Publication Data

Lutz, Giles A.
    The Trespassers / Giles Lutz.--Center Point large print ed.
        p. cm.
    ISBN-13: 978-1-60285-068-2 (lib. bdg. : alk. paper)
    1. Large type books. I. Title.

PS3562.U83T74 2007
813'.54--dc22

2007018512

07-2264
Centerpoint
12/07
29.95

Chapter One

It was a raw, late October morning, and the big man, driving the wagon, cursed the pelting rain. This was the third such day of it, and it was more than enough. His hat brim had lost its stiffening. It drooped against the back of his neck allowing the water to pry at the neck of his slicker with sly, persistent fingers. Some of those fingers found entrance and trickled down inside the slicker, wetting Verl Wakeman's shirt and chilling him. This rain would have been welcome a couple of months ago, but now it would hamper the corn harvest. Fields dried slowly in late fall, and only a hard freeze would make them passable for teams and wagons. And a hard freeze this early presaged a long and cold winter.

Verl grinned sourly. A man could curse the weather until he was black in the face, and it did no good—except to release the inward pressure that threatened to tear him apart.

The team slogged through the deep, holding mud, and Verl made no attempt to hurry them. The horses wanted to get out of this weather as badly as he did, and they picked the pace best suited for it. He was a big man with broad, sloping shoulders and a deep chest that spoke of both endurance and power. His face was almost somber in repose, but a slow-spreading grin could transform it and wipe away the look of maturity the somberness gave it. He laughed often, for youth could find much to laugh at, and the laughter made his gray eyes dance. He was twenty-three years old and in the full swell of his prowess. He wasn't a handsome man in any sense. His mouth was too big, his nose too prominent. Its lopsided appearance, caused by an early fight, didn't enhance it. But women were attracted to him, perhaps drawn by the inner vitality of the man. He found a complacent content with his lot. He and his father owned three hundred acres of the finest Grand River bottomland, and most of it was cleared. Many a felled tree had gone into putting that thickness in his chest and the bulge in his arms.

He glanced at the old Avery place as he passed it. When the trees were in leaf, the house couldn't be seen. But the rain had stripped most of the dead leaves from their branches, and the house stood forlorn and desolate-looking on its little knoll. The house had been empty for the last five years while old Avery's heirs had wrangled in court. An inheritance brought out the vultures, Verl thought, and grimaced. Brother turned against sister where money was involved, and their claws and beaks were longer than any carrion bird's.

But the case had been settled and the Avery farm sold. The new buyer had moved in last week. Verl had called, offering any possible help. He turned Verl away with a stiff courtesy that couldn't be penetrated.

Verl's face was tight at the memory of it. He hadn't been invited inside the house, nor offered the least of the common hospitalities. Well it'd be a cold day in hell before Verl ever offered the bearded man anything. His damned house could burn down and Verl would stand by and watch it.

It was a bad thing when a standoffish man moved into the country. A man needed good neighbors, and he offered help and received it with equal ease. He'll learn, Verl thought, dismissing the bearded man from his thoughts.

The hill ahead was a bad one, and he put his attention on his driving. He braked and took up the slack in the reins, holding the team back. Each time they took a step the hoofs slid, and they snorted at the uncertain footing. The heavy wagon pushing at their heels didn't help settle them down.

Verl stood up in the box cursing the man who had engineered this road. It was crowned in the middle, and a deep ditch ran on each side of it. He tried to straddle the crown but the yellow clay kept sliding beneath his wheels. The muscles in his arms bulged as he tried to hold the team back. It could be a losing cause. He might have to let the team have their heads and hope they could outrun the wagon.

Halfway down, the wagon jackknifed and the back end slid toward the ditch. He yelled at the team and lashed them, hoping to get enough foot out of them to jerk the wagon back into line. But the incline of the road had the wagon, and the greasy clay furnished no traction. Hoofs slashed at the road but they couldn't get enough purchase to slow or stop the wagon's skid.

It was going into the ditch and nothing Verl nor the team could do would prevent it.

He tried to jump but the wagon box was canted precariously and he could get no springboard. His foot slipped, a knee slammed into the floor boards.

He yelled hoarsely as a rear wheel dropped into the ditch. The off wheel rose higher and higher, tilting the wagon to a perilous degree. He tried to scramble up the inclined floor; his fingers slid along it without finding a hold. The horses screamed in shrill fright, and Verl heard the slam of their hoofs as they fought to keep from being dragged into the ditch. The twisting motion of the wagon and the angle of the team put too severe a strain on the tongue and it snapped. The team lurched forward and the tugs parted. At least the team wouldn't be pulled into the crackup.

Without the drag of the team there was nothing to keep the wagon from going over. Its timbers creaked and groaned as it reached the apex of its tilt. Verl tried to spring clear of it but he was on the wrong side of the angle. He had only one way to go, the ditch side, and he doubted he could get enough momentum to clear the overturning wagon. He tried. He threw his body to the ditch side, pushing hard with his arms to get enough force to clear the wagon. He landed face down and slid toward the bottom. A great, black weight was falling toward him, blotting out the sky. It hit him across the shoulders jamming his face into the mud. Something seemed to burst inside his skull and he knew no more.

He didn't want to open his eyes. He knew it would take tremendous effort, and the effort would demand its price in pain.

He opened his eyes and groaned. He was right about what the effort cost him. The pain slammed at him in waves, and he set his teeth hard against it. A weight seemed to be crushing him and he couldn't understand it. It came back to him slowly, a small segment at a time. He remembered the wagon sliding toward the ditch and its slow overturning. He was pinned beneath it and he lay on one arm. He tried to free the arm and the weight pressing down on his body was too great. His efforts brought the pain back again and he wondered how badly he was smashed up.

He lay there, waiting for the pain to abate. At its peak it was a dizzying, blinding thing, and unless it retreated he wouldn't even be able to think calmly.

He shut his eyes until the sharp lancing subsided into a dull prodding. He would waste no more strength in frantic, uncoordinated effort. He had a wagon on top of him but one arm was free. Surely he should be able to get enough leverage to raise that weight and wriggle free.

He waited until his breathing returned to normal then propped the free elbow under the wagon's edge. He put his palm against the slippery earth and tried to raise the weight. His palm was against the cut of the ditch and each time he put force into the arm the palm slid. He swore at the mud and the resisting weight, at first in anger then with increasing fear. The cold, wet touch of the sodden earth was penetrating his body and his teeth chattered against the chill. He said aloud, "Maybe you'd better yell. Somebody might hear you." The sound of his voice was comforting even while logic pointed out that yelling probably wouldn't do him any good. But this was a main-traveled road to Gallatin. In ordinary weather somebody passed along it every so often. But this wasn't ordinary weather, and few people would venture out into it unless necessity drove them. He should have listened to his father. Anse had said he was crazy to go out in this rain. But Verl had wanted to see Elly. He thought with grim humor that Anse would have some very pointed things to say about his hard-headedness.

He yelled with all the strength of his lungs, spacing the yells at two- to three-minute intervals. He yelled until his voice hoarsened then faded into a faint squawk.

He waited for strength to return again, trying to keep his thoughts clear and rational. It seemed darker than he remembered it before the wagon overturned and he wondered about it. It hit him hard that he had probably been unconscious for a long time. The coming darkness lessened his chances that somebody might pass along the road. Verl began to panic, but he fought against its grip. The panic hammered at him with relentless force: he would never survive the exposure of a night here.

He yelled again, not from hope, but because it was

the only effort he could make. The rain mocked him with its steady drumming.

He thought dully, one more time. Just one more. He yelled—a sublime effort that should have been heard clear to Gallatin.

He lifted his head as he thought he heard a voice. It must be the rain mocking him. But no, he was certain he heard it this time. He yelled with renewed vigor.

He could hear the sliding progress as something came slithering down the ditch. Then big, round, blue eyes looked at him and a shaky voice asked, "Mister, are you alive?"

Verl had never seen an angel, but this would do until one came along. The boy appeared to be in his mid-teens, skinny, with frail arms.

"See if you can get this wagon off me," Verl grunted.

The boy tried. He gripped the edge of the bed and strained until he was red in the face. He didn't budge the weight.

"I'm sorry, mister." He looked as though he were about to cry.

"Find a pole. Maybe you can pry it up."

The boy's face brightened and he nodded. It seemed an eternity before he came back with a six-foot pole. He put one end under the wagon and his shoulder under the other. He strained until his knees began to shake.

"I can't," he wailed.

Verl wanted to rave at him. Why did it have to be

this frail, skinny kid who came along? He had been straining with the boy, and he was exhausted.

He said, "Maybe you'd better go and get some help." His chattering teeth were shaking and distorting his words. "Hurry, boy."

"I will," the youth promised and scrambled up the bank.

Verl learned the meaning of loneliness. The minutes dragged by on leaden feet. He cursed the boy's dawdling, and frightening thoughts prodded and poked at him. How far did the boy have to go, or had he given up the idea entirely, deciding he could do nothing about it? Verl cursed the thoughts. His shaking was a physical violence. Even his bones ached with the cold. Then he suddenly felt hot as though he were being roasted alive.

Delirium, he thought. How could a man be so cold one minute then so hot the next? He didn't know. Nothing made any difference now. The boy wasn't going to return in time. Maybe there hadn't been a boy. Maybe that was part of the delirium. A black void was reaching for him and he fought it off. He tumbled faster and faster toward that black void and his efforts to stop his plummeting were useless. He shut his eyes and let go. It was a lot more pleasant than all that useless effort.

Chapter Two

Verl opened his eyes and looked about the strange room. It was furnished austerely, but the feather bed was thick and comfortable. It must be morning for light filled the room. What had happened between the time he remembered and now? For a moment he considered that he had died and gone to the other world the preachers were always talking about. The better one, he amended and grinned. He did remember a few moments during the night but they must have been dreams and not lucid moments. He had cursed the chills that shook him so violently and a girl had placed her fingers across his lips. The touch of those fingers had been cool and soothing. She had red-gold hair and the biggest blue eyes he had ever seen. He remembered trying to touch that face, and she had retreated from him.

Yes, he decided and sighed. It was all a dream, and he wished it weren't. The beauty of that girl's face would haunt him forever. He wondered where he was but was too tired to be much concerned about it.

A voice said from the doorway: "So you decided to wake up." Verl turned his head. The bearded man, the one who had moved onto the old Avery place, stood in the doorway. His eyes held neither hostility nor friendliness.

"Am I at the Avery place?" Verl asked.

"My place now," the man corrected. "It was the old Avery place."

Verl kept his irritation in check. This man must have gotten him out of the ditch and now Verl owed him a lot. But he was too touchy about his ownership. It would be years before this farm would be called anything other than the Avery place.

Verl said, "I'm grateful to you."

The man nodded. Every motion he made, every word seemed to be guarded, and Verl wondered what had put him so on the defensive.

"Blaine came running home last evening yelling a man was in the ditch. He was so excited he could hardly talk. When he said you were pinned down by a wagon I took time to harness up the team. It took the team to drag the wagon off you."

"The cold was getting to me," Verl said gravely. "I don't think I would have made it through the night."

A faint grin touched the man's face. "We piled quilts on you, and still you cursed us for not bringing more."

"I regret that."

"It's understandable," the man said dryly. "Heather," he called. "He's awake. You can bring him some breakfast."

Verl heard the light tap of footsteps, and the girl appeared in the doorway carrying a tray. So it hadn't been a dream. The girl was real. Her eyes were the blue of a clear May morning, and fathomless in their depths. He couldn't help staring openly at her. He judged her to be seventeen, not over eighteen at the most, and she was sweetly formed. She wore a man's shirt, much too large for her, and even its

14

shapelessness couldn't hide the femininity under it.

His eyes kept going over her face like searching fingers, and she colored under it.

He said, "I've just been told I made quite a show of myself."

She laughed, and the sound was like the tinkling notes of a tapped crystal glass. "You gave us trouble," she said.

He looked at the nightshirt he wore and said in alarm, "You didn't—"

The color deepened in her face. "Blaine and father got the wet clothes off you. They had quite a struggle."

He grinned and said, "For a moment I was afraid—" He broke off, and now the color was in his face.

She wouldn't meet his eyes as she asked, "Can you sit up?"

He tried to use his left arm to prop himself up, and grunted as a stab of pain shot through his shoulder. His right hand went to the spot; the shoulder felt swollen. He knew it was sensitive.

"Maybe I'd better feed you," she said.

Her eyes touched his then skipped lightly away. She reminded him of a doe, wanting to draw closer but poised to flee. His heart was beating much too fast for just lying in bed.

"I think you'd better," he said.

She sat the tray beside him and fed him a spoonful of the hot mush. It was laced with dollops of thick, yellow cream, and he had never tasted anything better.

The bearded man watched with disapproving eyes. "We didn't know who you were," he said.

Verl thought, You would have, if you had been more friendly the other day. He pushed the ungrateful thought aside. "Verl Wakeman. My father and I own land a couple of miles from here. We're practically neighbors."

"Don't talk," the girl said, and fed him another spoonful.

He smiled at her. They were going to be the best of neighbors. He would see to that.

"I'll send Blaine to notify your father you're here," her father said. "Blaine," he called.

The boy had to be standing just outside the door to appear so quickly. He looked at his father first and said, "Yes, sir?" He stole a covert glance at Verl.

"You'll have to give him directions," the man said.

It released the boy's attention to Verl and he said eagerly, "You look better than you did last night." He grinned, showing an easy, outgoing nature. "Boy, did you fight us."

Verl returned the grin. "I'm sorry about that, Blaine." His face sobered. "You know you saved my life, don't you?"

Blaine dug his toe into the floor and said, "Aw, I didn't do much." His eyes were shining.

Verl's teeth flashed. "It was pretty important to me." He would have to do something pretty special for this boy.

The man said impatiently, "If you will give him directions—"

16

Verl glanced at him. The man was certainly extending only the most grudging hospitality. He told Blaine how to reach the Wakeman farm and said, "Tell Anse I'm all right."

"Shouldn't he tell your father to bring a buggy or something?" the man asked. At Verl's surprised look he said, "I thought you'd like to go home as soon as possible."

"Father," Heather cried. "He may be hurt badly." She blushed under her father's probing look. "I thought he shouldn't leave for another day at least."

"Can you travel?" the man asked bluntly.

The shoulder was sore, and Verl felt bruised and battered all over. But the man didn't want him here any longer than he had to be.

He said curtly. "I can travel." He wondered if this man was unfriendly by nature or if he was hiding something. He looked at Blaine and said, "Tell Anse to bring another horse."

Blaine nodded and bolted out of the room.

Some kind of rebellion was in the girl's face, and Verl smiled at her. She wanted him to stay.

"I'm all right," he said. He would leave today but he would be back shortly.

Her father asked pointedly, "Heather, haven't you work to do?"

"Yes," she said. Her eyes met Verl's for a fleeting instant, then she turned and walked out of the room.

Verl said, "I still don't know who to thank." If the man didn't give his name this time Verl intended asking for it openly.

The man's tone was reluctant. "Phelps. Micajah Phelps. You owe us no thanks."

"I'm in your debt, and I'll repay it."

Phelps shook his head with a dogged insistence. "There is no debt."

"And I feel there is," Verl snapped. There could readily be open hostility between them, and he couldn't understand why. Blaine and Heather accepted him but Phelps didn't. Was there something about his appearance that rubbed Phelps raw?

"Have it your way," Phelps said and left the room.

Verl kept hoping Heather would return but she didn't. He consoled himself with the thought that she wanted to but didn't because of her father. It was apparent Phelps held dominion over this household.

He squirmed, trying to find a more comfortable position, and the movement sent a stab of pain through his shoulder. He probed at it with delicate fingers. It was sore enough to be a broken bone. Now wouldn't that be a hell of a note with all the work ahead of him?

He half turned and looked out the window. The rain had stopped, but the sky was still overcast. The earth looked soggy with moisture. He counted the cracks in the ceiling, he looked at the scoured floor. The Avery place had been in pretty bad shape the last time he had seen it. If this room was an example Phelps and his family had done wonders with the house.

What in the hell was keeping Anse. He thought of calling Heather but couldn't determine on a plausible excuse.

He had just decided excuse be damned when she came into the room. She carried his clothes and she laid them at the foot of the bed.

She said, "There wasn't time to wash them. But they're dry."

He noticed she had also scraped the mud from them. He said, "Thank you." He thought some new constraint was in her. If so, it had to be from something Phelps said to her. Maybe Phelps was standing just outside the door, and he grinned faintly at the sour thought.

He wanted to keep her. "I'm glad you moved here," he said.

She kept her face turned from him, and he saw the color wash up her throat and spread through her cheek. She gave him a quick, startled look, then almost fled the room.

The church box supper was next week, and he wondered what she'd say if he asked her to go with him. But maybe it was too early to tender that kind of an invitation.

The minutes resumed their slow parading. He thought, to hell with it, and sat up. He ignored the protest his shoulder made. He was angry at Anse for being so late, at Phelps for his unfriendliness, at Heather for not talking to him. He would dress and walk home.

He thought, You're working yourself up pretty good. Maybe Phelps acted in the best light of the circumstances. After all he was Heather's father. Didn't that entitle him to a little consideration? Verl thought soberly, a lot of consideration.

He thought he heard voices downstairs and strained in an effort to catch words. He heard a heavy, gruff voice ask, "Where is he?" and his face brightened.

"Anse," he yelled. "I'm up here."

He heard the ponderous steps. Stairs always brought out Anse's fifty-seven years.

Anse was puffing as he came into the room. He was a big man, though he lacked Verl's height. He had the same craggy face, but lined more deeply with the tracery of the years. One could look at these two and know they were close kin. Anse had given Verl a splendid heritage of size and strength. He was still a good man though he tired more readily than he used to. But he was still the boss, and Verl made no mistake about it.

Verl jeered, "You don't carry that stomach so well up stairs."

He felt a tremendous affection for his father, though the remark didn't show it. He was twelve when his mother died, and Anse had raised him unaided. He'd done quite a job of it, despite Verl's aunts' protestations that it just wasn't right. A young boy needed a woman's softening influence or he was bound to grow up coarse and tough.

Verl had grown up tough all right. But it was a toughness of mental outlook, rather than spirit. Anse had demanded that. When a man took hold of a situation he hung onto it regardless of how it whipped him

20

around. He taught him other valuable lessons. He taught him the value of hard work and of honesty. Anse's favorite remark was, "When a man's honest he can look anybody in the eye. Do your best and make no apology to anybody. Not even yourself." Only once had Verl lied to his father, and Anse had caught him in it.

"That's a lie, son," Anse said.

"No," Verl insisted stubbornly.

That was the backing for the first lie, and he got his whipping for it. A leather strap had a way of teaching lessons that a boy never forgot. It was funny: he could still remember the whipping though he couldn't remember what the lie had been about.

Anse did a poor job of hiding the concern in his eyes. "You all right?" he asked gruffly.

"You took your time getting here to find out."

"Doc Courtney was at the house. You know how slow he is."

"What did you bring him for?" Verl yelled. "I can tell you I'm all right."

"I'll let him make sure. Hey, Doc," he called. "Are you coming up?"

Courtney's voice floated up the stair well. "Be right there." Courtney was another man of considerable weight, and Verl heard the stair timbers creak.

Anse said, "The boy gave quite an account of your accident."

Verl shook his head. "He built it up. Did the team come home?"

"After dark. I did some riding but couldn't find you. You know I passed that wagon and didn't see it."

"I'm sorry, Anse." Anse had had some bad hours riding in the wet blackness. "Is the wagon smashed up?"

"It'll take some mending," Anse said dryly.

Courtney came into the room. He was florid-faced. A ring of white hair set off his ruddy pate. His blue eyes were faded, and he wheezed as he walked. He was always complaining about this damned climate not letting a man breathe. He had brought Verl into this world, and seen him through the common childhood diseases. Most of the men in the county of Verl's age could say the same thing.

Courtney said, "Tried to break your fool neck, didn't you? And here I was planning on sitting before the fire all day. I could lose all my patients and still make a living if I had you left."

"That's a lie," Anse said hotly. "I never raised no sickly boy."

Courtney cackled. "Look at him. All I need to do to get a rise out of him is to tell him how puny you are."

Anse said, "That's because you're so damned unhealthy. You can't stand seeing anybody healthy."

Verl grinned. These two were the best of friends. They were at each other's throat every time they met.

"See if he broke anything," Anse ordered.

"You telling me my business?" Courtney demanded.

"Will you stop that," Verl snapped. "I want to get out of here."

Courtney was thorough in his examination. He

poked and prodded, and each movement was accompanied by a hem or a haw.

Anse watched everything Courtney did. He tried to disguise his worried interest by asking, "How'd it happen, Verl?"

"The wagon jackknifed on me. I tried to jump before it went over. It caught me."

Courtney's fingers were on Verl's sensitive shoulder. He saw Verl's wince and said, "Hah."

He pressed harder, and Verl swore at him.

"Hurts, huh?"

Verl said sourly, "The way you handle a patient, I'm surprised any of them lived."

Courtney glanced at Anse. "He gets that tongue from you."

Anse ignored the thrust. "Is it broken?"

Courtney shook his head. "Don't think so." He moved the shoulder, and Verl found a new cuss word. "Just dislocated," Courtney said. "It'll be at least a week before he's back at work."

Anse shook his head. "He can find more ways to get out of work. First, he gets elected captain of his militia company. Then he takes a job as honorary deputy. Now this."

Courtney missed the relief in Anse's eyes. "You ought to be grateful it's no worse. If he didn't have the constitution of an ox he'd have caught pneumonia, lying out in that ditch as long as he did. He's going to need help dressing."

Verl found out how right Courtney was. He insisted

on slipping into his left shirt sleeve despite Courtney's advice to let it flap. Each time he moved that shoulder it screamed at him and beads of sweat popped out on his forehead.

"You ready to listen to me?" Courtney demanded tartly.

Verl nodded and grinned weakly.

Courtney said, "I'll have to get something for a sling. Maybe I can borrow a dish towel." He waddled toward the door.

"Anse, I'm sorry about the wagon."

Anse glared at him. "Did you do it on purpose?" He shook his head. "We'll get it fixed up. Forget about it." He turned his head toward the door; his eyes were thoughtful. "Odd family," he said.

"The father is."

Anse conceded the point. "He didn't seem to even want to give me his name. The boy was friendly enough."

Verl waited then asked in exasperation. "Did you see the girl?"

Anse gave him a veiled glance. "I did. What about her?"

"Of all the damned-fool questions. She's the prettiest thing I ever laid eyes on."

Anse gave him a long, reflective survey. "She's pretty enough," he agreed. "But it looks to me like somebody's stepped on her spirit."

Before Verl could reply Courtney came back into the room. He carried a dish towel, and he fashioned a sling out of it.

Verl kept thinking, Anse is wrong about her not having any spirit. He should have heard her laugh.

Courtney adjusted the sling and asked, "How's that feel?"

"Better," Verl answered. It was much better. With the weight of the arm supported it took the ache out of the shoulder.

He found out how helpless a one-armed man is. They had to help him dress. Anse buttoned Verl's shirt over the arm in the sling. The dangling left sleeve was an indignity.

Courtney straightened after helping Verl tug on his boots. "He's pretty helpless, isn't he?"

"Yep," Anse said. "I guess I got him where I want him."

Verl glared at them and walked toward the door. He winced at the first few steps. He was pretty battered. But motion drove some of the stiffness away and he was steady enough as he went down the stairs.

The Phelps family was in the kitchen.

Verl said, "I'll never forget what you did for me." He took Heather's hand and held it until he was aware of Phelps' frown.

He released her hand and tousled Blaine's hair. The boy beamed at him in delight.

"And you," Verl said. "I'll make it up to you."

"It isn't necessary," Phelps said stiffly.

Verl didn't offer to shake hands with him. He had the feeling that at best Phelps wouldn't like it. And he might even refuse the proffered hand.

He went out the door, and Anse and Courtney followed him. Anse looked back toward the house. "There'll never be much neighboring between us."

Anse was wrong about that, Verl vowed. He was coming back here. And he'd win Phelps over.

Anse helped Verl up into Courtney's buggy. He repeated a question three times before Verl heard it.

"Damn it, Verl," Anse snapped.

"I didn't hear you," Verl said, and colored. Anse's eyes made him feel guilty as hell about something. Courtney was so busy getting his old, tired mare into motion, he didn't notice a thing.

Chapter Three

Anse stepped back and surveyed his work. He had fashioned a new tongue out of a seasoned pole of red elm. Red elm was a hard, durable wood, defying tools until a man's patience wore thin. But when he finished he had something that would last.

Verl had tried to help, but he was sure he had been more a hindrance. If he ever saw a one-armed man again he would give him every consideration.

"That's about all we can do with it," Anse grunted. "We're going to have to drag it into town and let Hoady work on it. I know the kingpin's bent."

He hitched up the team and threw two saddles into the wagon bed. They would ride the team back, leaving the wagon with Hoady.

He offered Verl a hand up into the box, and Verl said, "Hell, I'm not helpless."

"I'm glad you told me. I'd never have known." He laughed at Verl's scowl.

He climbed up beside Verl and picked up the reins. He drove slowly, his head cocked to one side. "Just as I thought," he grunted. "She's not tracking worth a damn."

Verl sat wrapped in his thoughts. It had been three days since his accident, and he hadn't gone near the Avery place. Oh, he wanted to. He had discarded one excuse after another. It would have to be a strong excuse, for he had to satisfy two people—Anse and Phelps.

Anse prodded him with an elbow. "Do you ever listen any more?"

The picture of Heather faded from Verl's mind. "What did you say?"

Anse frowned. "I wish I knew where you go the last few days. I said, it looks like we've got a bad winter coming."

"Why?"

Anse pointed overhead. A long V of geese winged southward, and their mournful honking drifted back to the earth. Something was really filling Verl's head for he usually spotted or heard the wild geese first.

Verl stared into the sky. A second V followed the first, then another. In a few moments the sky seemed full of geese. The wild geese always stirred some atavistic instinct in him, filling him with a sad wistfulness. Maybe it was because he was earthbound, and the geese weren't. He never tried to explain it beyond that.

Anse said, "They're coming through early. Looks like a mean winter ahead."

Verl was afraid Anse was right. The wild geese knew—and they fled before the onslaught of long, savage cold. Nothing could be meaner than a north Missouri winter.

He said, "I'd better be getting on that woodpile."

"You won't with that shoulder," Anse disagreed. "We got time enough."

Verl nodded and was silent. He wondered if Phelps was prepared for a rough winter. He wished his shoulder was mended. He'd help Phelps with his winter's supply of wood. He grinned suddenly. That was a sure way to win a man over—help him with the chore of chopping and sawing wood.

"What are you grinning about?" Anse asked.

"Nothing."

Anse frowned at him. From time to time he put little, covert glances on Verl. But he didn't pry.

They drove down the main street of Gallatin, and people waved and called to them. Very few people had enmity for either Verl or Anse Wakeman. Too many could tell of a helping hand from those two.

Gallatin wasn't a big town. Less than forty houses surrounded the half-dozen business establishments. But it was the county seat of Daviees and important for that reason.

Anse pulled up before the blacksmith shop. He said too casually, "I can talk to Hoady about the wagon if you want to see Elly."

"Maybe later."

The frown returned to Anse's face. Elly was no raving beauty, but a man was foolish to marry for that reason alone. The beauty faded first, and if there was nothing left a man was bankrupt in his marriage. Elly had other, greater, assets. There was a sweetness to her nature: a man would have to go a long way to find its equal. Verl had never said he was serious about her, but Anse assumed he was. When a man went with a girl for six months, one just sort of concluded some feeling was between them. How Elly felt about Verl showed every time she looked at him. Did that Phelps girl have something to do with Verl's complete lack of interest today? Anse's frown deepened. It couldn't be. Verl had seen her only once. A man didn't throw away something tested because of a brief exposure like that.

His thoughts must have been showing for Verl said softly, "It's my business, Anse."

Anse sighed. Verl was absolutely right. A man had to do the important job of selecting a woman by himself, yet people kept insisting upon meddling in it. It was an easy trap to step into.

He followed Verl into the blacksmith shop. Two men were there besides Hoady. Hoady said, "Howdy, Anse. Verl." He pumped a bellows and the embers in his forge sprang into licking life. He had powerful arms, and the flames gave a ruddy joviality to his face.

Britton and Atterbury crowded close to the forge, for

29

beyond the fire's reach the air was nippy. Sometimes Verl envied them. They seemed to have so much idle time on their hands.

Hoady tonged a glowing shoe from the forge and moved with it to an anvil. He brushed Britton and said, "Will you loafers get out from under foot?"

Britton grinned. "He hates to have to work while the rest of us sit." He was a lank man with broken teeth. Sitting was the best thing he did. In the summer it was fishing; in the winter it was near somebody's fire. Verl didn't like the man. When a man borrowed firewood, with all the timber around just for the cutting, he was pretty damned lazy. Britton always had an excuse—if his axe wasn't broken, his saw was. He was a borrowing, non-returning man.

Hoady ignored Britton's remark. "How's the arm, Verl?"

"Coming along. You heard about my accident?"

Hoady grinned, displaying big, white teeth. "Doc Courtney's told everybody how he snatched you right out of the jaws of death."

"Oh hell," Verl grunted.

"We brought the wagon in, Hoady," Anse said. "It needs some work on the running gear. Can you get at it?"

Hoady laid down the shoe. "I'll take a look at it." People were always pulling him off his present job. He stepped outside, and everybody followed him. He stooped and inspected the running gear. "The kingpin's bent."

"I know that," Anse said. "How long will it take to fix it?"

Hoady scowled in concentration. He was a slow, deliberate man and he fought anybody pushing him. "I'll have to jerk the bed off. It'll take some time."

"How long?" Anse insisted.

"We'd like to get in the corn fields, Hoady," Verl said. "Just as soon as they dry up."

It eased the frown on Hoady's face. "Three or four days. No sooner."

Anse nodded. His pleasure showed in his eyes. He hadn't really expected the wagon in less than a week. He and Verl had worked on Hoady before. One pushed and the other soothed Hoady's ruffled feelings.

Britton snickered. "I'll bet you were drunk, Verl."

Verl swung cold eyes to him. "Why?"

"A man has to be drunk to drive a wagon off the road like you did."

"He wasn't drunk," Anse snapped.

"Hell, Anse," Britton protested. "I was just funning him." He wanted to get the fire out of Anse's eyes and he said lamely, "I wish my wagon was ready so I could start shucking. It's got a broken wheel."

Hoady said, "I told you to bring it in three weeks ago." He turned back to the shop without waiting for Britton's answer. He had heard too often about how busy Britton was.

The others followed him and took comfortable positions near the fire.

"Your corn good, Verl?" Britton asked.

31

"Guessing it at sixty bushels or better."

Britton sighed in envy. "Mine didn't do a God damned thing."

Verl could have pointed out that after planting Britton hadn't touched his fields. The weeds grew as fast as the corn. A man couldn't expect to get a yield by dropping a seed into the ground and leaving it untended. He held his judgment. He would only be wasting his breath.

Atterbury said, "The old lady should be through shopping by now. I'd better be picking her up." He stood and walked to the door. He opened it and stared out into the street.

"I'll be damned," he said softly. "More of them. Will they ever quit coming?"

The others crowded behind him and looked over his shoulder. A pitiful file of people trudged down Gallatin's street. A dozen men were bent laboriously behind push carts, piled high with family possessions. Women walked beside them, carrying youngsters too small to toddle. The older children walked beside their mothers, some of them clutching at skirts for support. If the boys were old enough they pushed at the handle of the carts alongside their fathers. The young girls carried bundles that couldn't go on the overcrowded carts.

Britton stared at the motley procession with malignant eyes and swore. "Haw long are we going to put up with it?" he demanded.

"Put up with what?" Verl asked absently. The mark

of many hard miles showed in those people's drooping shoulders, in the muscle-weary slack of their bodies. Pushing those carts through the holding mud was a taxing thing. But their heads were up and their faces calm. It took determination to ignore the weariness they must have felt.

"I see them pass almost every day," Hoady said soberly. "All heading for Caldwell County, going to their second Zion. I wonder what they see that keeps pushing them on."

"They see lies," Britton said hotly. "They listen to that damned Joseph Smith."

"They must believe him," Verl said dryly. Some people called the Mormon coming an invasion and cursed it as bitterly as Britton did. A minority defended them, saying they were thrifty, hardworking people minding their own business. You rarely found anybody neutral on the subject. "How would you stop it, Britton?" he asked.

Britton's eyes swung from face to face. "They're trespassers," he said heatedly. "They ought to be treated that way. Run them out of the country—or kill them."

Verl couldn't resist the temptation to goad this ignorant, shiftless man, a man resentful of good fortune that came to others through hard work. He said, "Boggs gave them Caldwell County. How are you going to run them off land that belongs to them?" Ray County had been split by official edict of the governor, and the northern portion of it renamed Caldwell

County. It was poor soil, and a man had to slave to force it to produce a living for himself and his family. It was a small miracle that the Mormons were doing it. Verl hadn't been to Far West, the Mormon's county seat, but he had heard it was a prospering town.

Britton hedged at Verl's opposition. "I wouldn't be objecting if they stayed in Caldwell. But they're spilling over into Daviees County. They're getting thick around Adam-on-Diamon. The Mormons say that Adam was born there. Do you believe that?"

Hoady said with dry humor, "If this was the original Garden of Eden it sure as hell has changed."

Verl didn't know where Adam was born and cared less. If the Mormons found anything in believing that it was, all right with him. What Britton said about the Mormons spilling over into surrounding counties was true. But there had been a control set up by law against that. Two thirds of the Gentiles, as the Mormons called nonbelievers, had to give consent.

He pointed that out to Britton, and Britton yelled, "They're occupying the land by fraud. They move onto it claiming they're not Mormons then vote to let the others in."

Verl said in disgust, "You're going to believe what you want."

Britton turned to Anse for support. "Anse, you're older than him. You got some sense." He overlooked the darkening in Verl's eyes. "Weren't they run out of Jackson County for the reasons I just been saying?"

"Yes," Anse admitted. "I guess they got pretty bad

over there. They rubbed men the wrong way by their claim to be the chosen people, that all nonbelievers were going to be crushed by them. That gets kinda hard to swallow."

Britton gave Verl a triumphant glance. "You're against them, aren't you, Anse?"

Anse said quietly, "I'm not against any man because of his belief. Until he starts interfering in mine."

"Do you believe their Joseph Smith talks to God?" Britton asked.

"I don't know." Anse chuckled dryly. "I wasn't there to hear it. But quite a few people evidently do believe it."

Verl said, "Anse, are you going to spend all day arguing with him? You can't change his mind."

Heat appeared in Anse's eyes. He hadn't been doing any of the arguing. He had only answered Britton's questions. He saw the grin lying back of Verl's eyes and almost laughed. That damned Verl started an argument, then stepped out of it leaving him to carry the brunt.

Verl started to move, and Britton stepped in front of him. He said, "I talked to a fellow who knew Smith back east. He said Smith was known as a drunk and a swindler. Is that the kind of a man you think ought to head up a new religion? Maybe only drunks and swindlers follow him."

The cover on Verl's temper was thin. Britton would argue all day about nothing. Verl said, "I don't give a good God damn. You go tell his followers what you know. Now get out of my way."

Verl was ready to push him out of the way when the door opened. A man ran into the shop and his haste and the frantic look on his face said that fear rode him hard. He stopped between Verl and Hoady and for a moment his trembling lips wouldn't let him speak.

"Don't let them take me back," he begged. "They almost got me at the edge of town."

It sounded like a job for the law, and Verl stepped in. He wished Sam Gilliam were here. Sam was the sheriff of Daviees County, and he had more practice in handling such matters. Verl was positive of one thing: nobody was taking this man until he knew what it was all about.

"Who's they?" he demanded.

"The Mormons. From Far West."

"Are you a Mormon?"

"I was. Not any more. I thought when I got out of Caldwell County I'd be safe. They kept right on after me."

"Did you kill somebody?"

The man shook his head.

"Steal something?"

"I'm not a thief." The indignation in his voice rang true.

"Then why do they want you?"

"They say I broke one of their laws. By God, they make so many a man doesn't know where he stands."

"What do they want you for?" Verl's eyes bored into the man. "You're going to tell me what I'm up against if you want help from me."

The man's eyes shifted before Verl's hard stare.

"They wanted me to marry the widow Crowley. She's twenty years older than me. I can't stand the sight of her. Besides, I got a wife. I'm not taking on another to support no matter what the bishop says."

Britton's eyes were round. "You got one wife and they want you to take another?"

The man nodded.

"How many wives can a Mormon have?"

"As many as he can support."

"Now ain't that the damnedest thing?" Britton said.

Verl glanced at Britton, his anger evident. Obviously Britton had never heard of polygamy, and was fascinated by the implications of it.

"And it's all legal?" Britton asked.

"It is if the church says so."

Britton's face showed he had more questions he wanted to ask.

Verl said, "Shut up, Britton." He looked at the man. "If you're telling me the truth I promise they won't take you."

"I'm telling the exact truth," the man said. "No one stands up to Joseph Smith or any of his bishops without being punished for it." His face became suddenly drawn at the sound of hoofs in the street. "That's them. They saw me come in here."

Anse saw the look on Verl's face and warned, "Verl, they were given the right to make their own laws and administer their own courts. Maybe you haven't got a right to interfere."

"Then I'll take it. If a man doesn't want to marry, I'd

say it's his right. He might get punished for it in Caldwell. He won't here. They're not going to take him until Sam hears about this."

Anse started to add something then gave it up. He knew that stubborn look on Verl's face.

"They won't take you," Verl promised the man. "At least not right now."

The door opened, and five men strode into the shop. The leader was tall and thin with an air of commanding power. He wore a full beard, and his eyes were a dead, slate color. All five men carried rifles. The slate-eyed man stopped within a few feet of Verl.

"Enoch," he said. He had a rough edge to his voice that grated on Verl's nerves. "You're coming back with us."

"No," Enoch shouted. "I'm getting out of this country. I'm getting clear away from you. I'm sorry I ever listened to any of you. I'm sorry I joined your church."

Those eyes bored deeper than stone drills. "You're coming."

Enoch beseeched Verl with his eyes. Verl said, "Maybe he isn't. Not until the sheriff hears about it."

Those eyes probed at Verl. "He broke our law."

"Maybe your law holds in Caldwell," Verl snapped. "And maybe it doesn't hold here. He stays here until I get some answers."

He saw the flame flicker in those blank eyes, a small lick of ugly, red light that grew until it filled the pupils.

The man leaned forward and asked softly, "Would you disobey the law of God?"

"I've got to know what that law is, first," Verl answered.

The man struck like a rattlesnake, without warning. Or maybe that flicker in his eyes was a warning too small for Verl to catch in time to protect himself. The disabled shoulder was a handicap. He saw the blur of the descending rifle barrel and threw up his arms. The barrel slashed across his skull before his arms were half raised. The blow set off whorls of bursting colors before his eyes. He thought he heard a high-pitched scream of fear as he fell forward on his face. He never felt the impact of the floor.

Chapter Four

He didn't want to open his eyes for he knew it would swing the door wide for the admission of pain. He knew pain already as a dull, throbbing ache but the light would be a whetstone, honing an edge on the pain until it was sword-keen.

He heard somebody say, "He's a long time coming around. It's a wonder his head isn't cracked."

The voice sounded familiar, and Verl wondered where he had heard it before. It was Anse who was talking, and Verl had the impulse to chuckle at how slow he had been.

He opened his eyes and closed them immediately. He was right about that edge. He waited until the pain quit slashing through his head then opened his eyes cautiously this time. The pain retreated. But it still waited for him to make an unwise move.

He looked at his father and mumbled. "What happened?" His eyes swept the room. It was strange to him. By the fripperies he would say it was a woman's room.

Anse's face was anxious. Hoady stood beside him with an equally concerned look.

"Don't you remember?" Anse asked. "He hit—"

The word "hit" was all Verl needed. The scene in the blacksmith shop came back instantly. He raised a hand to his head. It was wrapped in a wet towel. Now how in the hell did that get there?

"He must've fetched me a good one," Verl grunted.

"Knocked you colder than a dead fish," Hoady said solemnly.

Verl seldom knew a rapid anger. It started slowly and consumed relentlessly until he was a raging fire. He could feel that fire building now.

"Where is he?" he demanded. He was lying on a bed, and its frills and softness made him uncomfortable. At least somebody had had enough sense to remove his boots. He started to sit up. That was an unwise move. Something banged a great drum in his head, and its resounding echo lanced through him.

"Ooof," he said and laid his head back on the pillow.

His anger clung to his question. "Where is he?" he repeated.

Hoady shifted uncomfortably. "He's gone. He took that Enoch with him."

Verl stared at him. "What do you mean, he's gone?"

"Good God, Verl," Hoady exploded. "They had five rifles on us. They'd have used them too. We didn't have a damned thing. Did you expect us to throw rocks at them?"

"So you just let them walk out."

Hoady's eyes were furious. "We were in no better position to stop them than you were."

It was a good point, and the hard push of Verl's anger subsided. "Where am I?"

"In Elly's room," Anse answered. "She came by just as we were carrying you outside. She insisted we bring you here."

Verl looked about the room again. It was the first time he had ever been in her bedroom.

The door opened, and Elly Gilliam came into the room. She held a crushed towel in her hand, and Verl saw a few drops fall from it.

He pulled the one from his head and flung it on the floor. "I don't want that."

She stopped at the bedside. She had magnificent eyes in a plain face. She was tall for a woman but proportioned well. He had never seen her excited about anything.

She placed the fresh towel on his head, and her hands were gentle but competent.

"Elly, I said—"

"I heard you. It'll ease the ache."

She wasn't bossy. She just took hold of a situation and what she did was usually right. Maybe it was her perpetual calmness that irritated him at times.

"Did you order me brought here?" he asked.

She nodded. "They were carrying you outside for some air. Should I have left you lying in the street?"

"I guess the whole town saw it," he growled.

Hoady asked, "What are you complaining about? We had to carry you." A malicious spark of laughter danced in his eyes. He owed Verl something for his criticism. "We had quite a procession following us. Grant Shelby made some funny remarks."

"He's not so funny," Elly sniffed.

Verl groaned inwardly. He must have made quite a picture. He and Shelby traveled paths headed for a direct collision. The animosity had existed since school days. It was odd that during all these years there had been only one direct clash between them. Verl's crooked nose came from that schoolboy fight. They had fought until they were both worn out and neither had really won. Did the memory of that inconclusive fight keep both of them walking softly? Verl didn't know. But they were competitive in everything they did. Everybody knew how Shelby felt about Elly. Verl even admitted that his first motive in going with her had been to cut out Shelby. He hoped she never found that out. But that was changed now, changed by his growing fondness for her. Not marriage fondness, he thought. He had all the time in the world to be thinking of that. He and Shelby were both captains of their respective militia companies, elected by popular vote of the men. Once those companies had served the effective purpose of defense, but now Verl felt they were sort of outdated. There hadn't been an Indian outbreak for years, and there was really no excuse to call out the men except to honor a visiting dignitary. Verl supposed men loved to put on a uniform and parade like young cocks. He had even suggested disbanding the company, and a hundred voices howled him down. Hoady's was the loudest. Hoady loved that uniform.

He swung his feet to the floor, ignoring the pounding drum in his head.

"You can't get up," Elly said.

"Can't I," he answered. He pulled on his boots and stood. The room tipped dizzily, and he closed his eyes. He felt Elly's arm go around him, and he glared at her. She had had him carried up the street for the whole town to see and laugh at.

"Is Sam at his office?" he asked.

"I guess so," she replied.

"Verl, you're not going to push it farther?" Anse said.

He looked at his son and shook his head. He had asked a foolish question.

Verl walked to the door. The floor kind of swayed under his feet. He said, "Thanks, Elly," and didn't mean it to sound so grudging.

Faint color touched her face. "Sure," she said quietly.

She was fun to be with, and he enjoyed her company, but so far it had gone no farther than that. He had always figured that it took time for a deeper feeling to grow. But now a new face had intruded upon his thoughts, and maybe the growing had stopped forever. He saw the look in her eyes and was angry at the feeling of guilt it brought him.

He left the house, Anse and Hoady at his heels. He said, "Anse, I'll meet you at Hoady's place. I've got to see Sam."

Anse sighed as he watched him leave. It was never easy for Verl to forget a knock.

Hoady watched Verl with speculative eyes. "He's moving fast, like he's real mad."

"You can count on that, Hoady."

"After Verl gets through that damned Mormon won't feel so free to come in here and knock people down."

Anse nodded. Hoady could also bet that Verl was going to pay off that debt—with a little interest.

Chapter Five

Grant Shelby and Britton were among the four men lounging against the front of the general store. Verl steeled himself for the comments he knew were coming. His head still pounded. It wouldn't be wise for them to go too far with those comments.

Shelby pushed off the wall and blocked Verl's passage. His lips were grinning but his eyes were malicious.

"Hey, Verl," he said. "You looked real pretty being carried up the street. Even I could admire you."

44

Verl heard the snickers from the other men. He was beginning to burn around the edges. He said, "That's enough, Shelby." One of these days, this matter between them had to come to a head.

Shelby was three inches shorter than Verl; he was a powerful man with long arms and great strength in oversized hands. Verl remembered one silly contest he and Shelby had been pushed into last summer. The talk had been about strength, and several men in Shelby's company had insisted that Shelby could break anything with his hands. The claim was refuted hotly by some of Verl's men. Before Verl could stop the argument he was competing with Shelby to see who could break the largest stick with his hands without snapping it across their knees. They had worked up from small branches to that last two-inch stick. Verl strained over it. It had a lot of resiliency and it fought him, bulging the cords in his neck. When he heard it snap he knew that was as far as he could go. Shelby had strained over the same-sized stick and his face had grown red with exertion and fury. He raised his knee finally and brought the stick savagely down upon it. His men yelled it wasn't a fair contest, that Shelby's stick had been the largest. But Shelby knew he had lost. It was in his eyes.

The memory of that contest and a dozen others was in Shelby's face. He had tight-set eyes over a hatchet blade of a nose. His lips were thin and set in a hard line. It took some touch of cruelty to really make him laugh.

He said, "I wish me and a few of my boys had been there. No damned Mormon would have walked out on us."

"You couldn't have stopped them. You didn't have your Indian suits on."

Shelby's company called itself the Delaware Amaraguns. They wore feathers and full-fledged Indian regalia in all of their military maneuvers. They whooped and carried on like savages too. Verl considered it as a lot of damned nonsense.

Shelby's face burned. "Are you criticizing my company?"

"Take it any way you want."

"We can outdo your company," Shelby sneered.

It was a weakening remark and both of them knew it. Shelby had no intention of pushing this to a head today.

Verl looked at him for a moment and then moved on down the street. He heard the laughter break out behind him. The anger still nibbled at the edges but he had it under control.

Sam Gilliam was just dismounting before his office as Verl approached. Gilliam saw Verl's face and held up his hand. "Don't you go dumping any more trouble on me until I've had a drink." He stalked into his office, and Verl followed him.

The office was small and furnished shabbily. One leg of the desk was broken off and replaced by a couple of bricks. Gilliam sat down in the chair behind the desk. Verl knew that other rickety chair. He was afraid to sit in it.

Gilliam opened a drawer and pulled out a bottle and two glasses. He blew on the glasses and wiped them on his sleeve. He was a small man with tired eyes in a gray face. His age was indeterminate. But he had been sheriff for as long as Verl could remember. Blowing on the glasses was as close as they ever got to being washed. Gilliam claimed the whisky would kill the germs or make them drunk. And nobody ever got hurt from a dead or drunk germ.

Verl said, "Whoa," as the level in his glass rose. He didn't come in here to get drunk.

Gilliam drained half his glass and sighed. "I needed that. How's the shoulder?"

Verl wasn't surprised at Gilliam knowing about the accident. Gilliam usually kept on top of things that happened in his county. He had offered Verl the deputy job four months ago, warning him it carried no pay. Verl had accepted it under Elly's gentle pushing. Maybe he liked the authority of being able to pin on a badge anytime he wanted to. The no pay was a fair enough proposition. There wasn't much to do either.

He sipped at his whisky. It wasn't good liquor. On Gilliam's pay it was a wonder he could afford even this lousy stuff. Elly had done a job of managing to stretch Gilliam's pay into a decent living. Gilliam had raised her, after Indians had killed her parents. Mention of his granddaughter was the one thing that could put a proud light in his eyes.

Gilliam's pay had to be low for there wasn't a great

47

deal of tax money. Taxes were twenty-five cents on a hundred dollars' valuation. Very few men paid as much as five dollars in taxes. A farmer was better off than a city man. He raised his own food and he had something to barter for other things he needed. Dressed pork was a dollar and twenty-five cents a hundred pounds. A good milk cow cost ten dollars, a horse forty, but they were both acquired by trade. Nobody ever mortgaged his property to secure a debt. A simple hand-signed note was sufficient.

Gilliam finished his glass. "I just got back from Cy Donnelly's place. His prize boar is missing."

"Stolen?"

"Cy claims so. He's yelling the Mormons took it. I couldn't find any tracks. I think it just wandered off into the woods."

He poured a half glass of whisky and stared moodily at it. "By God, I'm getting a lot of complaints like that these days."

"All against the Mormons?"

Gilliam gave him a veiled glance. "Everybody says it's them."

"But you don't think so."

Gilliam's voice held an irritable note. "I'm not saying anything until I get some proof. But there's a hell of a lot of smoke being raised. People are getting themselves real worked up."

"I've got another complaint." Verl told him about the scene in Hoady's shop. "They took him with them," he finished.

Gilliam's eyes turned hard. "They got a lot of gall to ride in here and take a man out. What do you figure on doing about it?"

"Nobody tries to split my head and gets away with it," Verl said hotly. "I'm riding to Far West tomorrow and talk to somebody about it."

Gilliam narrowed his eyes. "I think I'd better ride over with you. Telling those people where they stand might save us a lot of trouble later on."

"You don't have to."

"You telling me how to run my office? I'm making this official business, Verl. I'll pick you up in the morning."

Chapter Six

In the morning, Anse watched Verl mount up. His eyes were troubled. He looked at Gilliam and said, "His shoulder is too sore for him to work. But he can go gallivanting all over the country."

Gilliam grinned at him. "Quit fretting over him. He's got me along to look after him." He chuckled at the wrath rushing into Anse's face. "We'd better leave, Verl. He knows a lot of bad words and he's about to use them on me."

Anse had no cause to worry. The shoulder was coming along faster than Courtney had said it would. Verl could still feel a twinge in it, but that stabbing pain was gone. "Be back as soon as I can, Anse." He touched his heels to the gelding's flanks.

A dozen southerly miles carried them into Caldwell County.

"We just crossed the county line," Gilliam said. "I haven't been here since before the Mormons came. I heard there's been a lot of changes."

"I used to hunt over here, Sam. There wasn't many people living around here."

"Shoal Creek's just ahead," Gilliam said. "We'll water the horses there."

Shoal Creek was dotted with settlements. Verl's mouth sagged in amazement. He saw mills, shops and stores and busy people at their tasks. They turned to stare at the two riders as they passed, and the faces were wooden.

"Not many people living here, huh?" Gilliam asked. His face was sober. "They flocked in here in a hurry, didn't they? We could ask some of them about our man, but we haven't even got a name to put to him. I think we'd better ride on to the county seat."

Verl felt the hostility in those blank-eyed stares. "I don't think they'd tell us anything," he said. "They look unfriendly. Is it because we're strangers or do they know we're not Mormons?"

Gilliam shrugged. He neither knew nor cared.

The farms seemed small but well-cared-for, and the harvested fields showed that the crops had been fairly good. These people had gotten as much out of this land as anybody could and more than most. In a half-dozen miles Verl hadn't seen a rundown place. He would have to give the Mormons credit for being hard-working and thrifty.

They topped a rise of ground, and Far West lay stretched out before them. Gilliam said, "Damn," and there was admiration in the oath. The town was bigger than Gallatin. These people had accomplished amazing things in a short time.

Verl judged the town site to be at least a square mile. It was laid out in blocks, each block appearing to be over a hundred yards square. He could see the four principal streets, each street seemingly wide enough for a dozen wagons abreast. Even the lesser streets had great width. Every street ran at right angles to a large public square, and there were signs of recent digging in it. He wondered why the square was so big and what they proposed erecting in it.

He sat there admiring the planning behind this town. It was excellent for it left room for growth, and the growth wouldn't overcrowd the original portion. He thought of Gallatin's narrow streets and haphazard building.

The same thoughts were running through Gilliam's mind for he grunted, "We could have borrowed something from them." He lifted the reins. "We might as well go on in."

When they reached the outskirts of the town, people came to their doors and stared at them.

Gilliam said irritably, "Are we that funny looking?"

Their way led down one of the wider streets, and Verl thought there must be well over a hundred houses in the town. Most of them were log cabins, but a few frame houses had been completed and others were starting. He passed two dry goods shops, three family grocery stores and a half-dozen blacksmith shops. This was a thriving town.

He commented on it, and Gilliam said, "It looks like they get things done. I wonder where the law is."

A man stood on the corner ahead of them, and Verl said, "We could ask him."

One thing paramount about these people was their reserve. This man had it too. He was stockily built, and his shoulders and hands said he was no stranger to hard work. He wore a full beard and what little of his face could be seen was weather-beaten. His eyes were blue with the sheen of ice on a cold January day.

"Are you looking for somebody?" he asked. His attitude showed he hadn't missed the badges, pinned to their shirts.

Gilliam gave Verl a warning glance. "Just looking," he said easily. "Mighty good-looking town you've got here."

The compliment thawed the man a little. "I would be proud to show it to you. You can lead your horses." He waited until they dismounted then said, "I'm Anderson. Ashel Anderson." He didn't offer to shake hands.

Verl introduced Gilliam, then himself. "It's a well-laid-out town," he said. "We were commenting on it as we rode in."

"The northern half of it is in my name," Anderson said.

Verl raised his eyebrows. That was a lot of valuable land for one man to own.

"All land here is held by our trustees," Anderson explained. "I am one of them."

A slight frown touched Verl's face. "How about the farms we passed?"

"If a man hasn't enough money to buy land, we buy it for him and hold it in the trustees' names. Such men are given forty acres to work." He pointed out a huge barnlike building. "The Lord's storehouse. All crops are stored there and portioned out fairly." He challenged Verl's frown. "You do not approve."

Verl shook his head. "It wouldn't do for me. It's too much like working for the other man."

"But we have no lazy nor needy people here."

That part of it was good, Verl admitted. But this system wouldn't do for him. A man would have to work a piece of land with somebody breathing down his neck and telling him how to work it.

"The Lord promised us this land," Anderson said with some firmness. "He gave it to all of us, and all of us work to make His gift bountiful. He has promised the whole earth, and some day he will give that to us, too."

Gilliam said dryly, "The state of Missouri had something to do with giving you this land. It partitioned Ray County."

"They were forced to by the Lord."

It was hard to reason with a man so set. Verl thought of the bottomland he and Anse worked. He said, "As to owning the whole world I expect you'll run into a little opposition."

Anderson said stiffly, "Each man has his own beliefs."

Verl nodded. "That's fair enough."

They approached the great open square. When they reached it Verl saw how extensive the digging had been. He whistled and said, "That's quite a hole. What's it for?" He looked into an open pit at least five feet deep and over a hundred feet long. Its width was almost equal to its length. It had taken a lot of man-hours to dig that hole.

"The foundation for our temple," Anderson answered. "One hundred and twenty feet long and eighty feet wide."

Verl looked at the two cornerstones already in place. They were fashioned out of great slabs of rock, and it had taken many muscles to move them. He said, "You put in quite a few days on that."

"One day," Anderson replied. At Verl's disbelieving look he said, "Five hundred men with mattocks and spades dug that from sunup to sundown. And hauled the dirt away in wheelbarrows."

Gilliam said, "It must have taken every able-bodied man in the county. Did they come willingly?"

"Why do you ask? Everybody works willingly for the Lord."

Gilliam said slowly, "I was just thinking that if they were ordered to work on this job it isn't a whole lot different than slave labor."

A sudden passion twisted Anderson's face. 'We do not believe in slave labor. Someday we will free all the slaves in this state. Then all over the world."

Gilliam said sourly, "You set yourselves ambitious projects." He exchanged glances with Verl, and Verl thought he knew what was on his mind. Missouri was a slave state, and much of the dislike of the Mormons by Missourians was caused by just such statements as Anderson had just made. The Wakemans owned no slaves, nor did they ever intend to. If the other man did that was his business. If Anderson was a fair sample of the Mormons Verl was beginning to understand their unpopularity.

He started to say something, and Anderson held up his hand. "Listen," he said.

Verl heard the faint throbbing of drums and the wailing of a fife.

Anderson's eyes fired as he said, "I thought it was time for the morning's drill." He stared in rapt attention toward the south entrance to the square.

The drums and fife grew louder, and a company of mounted men trotted into the square. Behind them were three companies of footmen, then another of horse. Verl watched them move into the square. He guessed five or six hundred men were under arms. Most of those arms looked new and the rest were in excellent condition. The men marched and wheeled about the square, obeying the barked commands of their officers.

Anderson's face was filled with a fanatic's zeal. Now Verl understood why the man had been so willing to show them the town. He had particularly wanted them to see this.

Gilliam put it bluntly. "You wanted us to see this. A threat?"

"Let's call it a warning," Anderson said quietly. "We can protect ourselves."

Verl thought, Missouri gave them the right to raise and command their own militia. That militia could be turned readily against Missourians.

A company front marched past them, and Anderson said, "That unit is led by Colonel Thunderbolt."

Verl glanced at him. That was an odd name, sounding almost Indian.

Anderson read the glance correctly. "All of our officers are named for the qualities they possess. We have a Colonel The Intrepid and a Captain Fear Not."

Verl wanted to laugh at the childishness of it, but Anderson's face was deadly serious.

"You may think those names are funny," Anderson said. "Some day you may find our officers are aptly named."

Verl was tired of the man's warnings. He started to say something, and Anderson said with evident satisfaction, "Here comes Captain Fear Not. He also leads our Danites."

Verl didn't know what the Danites were and cared less. He swung his eyes to the marching men. The man he was looking for led them.

He yelled in an excess of sudden rage. "That's him, Sam. That's the one."

He bounded into the square, paying no attention to

56

Anderson's startled cry. He heard the pound of Gilliam's feet as he followed.

He stopped in front of Captain Fear Not, blocking his way. The marching formations were thrown into confusion. Men piled up behind the Captain and those in front turned and came hurrying back. Verl and Gilliam were ringed by a thick pack of hostile faces.

In his anger Verl was blind to them. "I've been looking for you."

The Captain's mouth moved in a faint smile. "Now that you've found me, what good does it do you?"

Verl looked around at the angry faces, suddenly very much aware of how helpless he and Gilliam were. No good at all, he conceded mentally.

Gilliam snapped, "You took a man out of our town illegally. What happened to him?"

"We do not recognize your law. He has been punished by our law. I could have broken your man's head." The Captain added the last as an afterthought.

Verl had his anger under control. He would guess that Enoch was dead. There wasn't anything he and Sam could do for the man—there was nothing they really could do here at all.

A woman pushed through the crowd of watching men and ran up to the Captain. She laid her hand on his arm and asked, "Mace, is there trouble?" A wife would look at her husband with just such an expression.

The Captain struck the hand from his arm. "No trouble," he said harshly. "This isn't any of your business, woman. Now get out of here."

Verl saw the woman's sick face and was sorry for her. He waited until the crowd swallowed her then said, "It might be a sorry day for you that you didn't break my head. Don't come into my country again."

He heard shouts of anger from the nearest men, and saw rage in the Captain's eyes. But the man held up his hand, restraining the others from pushing forward at Verl and Gilliam.

"I could give you the same advice," he said. "Now get out of our country."

They locked eyes for a long moment, and Verl felt Gilliam's hand on his arm. He said curtly, "Your day." He turned and men parted to give him passage. He strode past Anderson, catching the satisfied smile on his face. The strangers had been taught an important lesson.

Verl and Gilliam walked to their horses and mounted. Verl looked back and the drilling had started again.

He said, "I'll run across him again some day."

Gilliam nodded. "It showed in both your faces." He said thoughtfully, "Maybe the people of Jackson County had their reasons. Right now I'd say these people are dangerous."

Chapter Seven

Anse said in shocked disbelief, "And you just turned and walked away from him?"

Verl's voice grew heated. "The odds were a little against us. About five hundred to two. I suppose you could have done something against those kind of odds."

58

"I wouldn't have put my tail between my legs and crawled off."

Gilliam saw the twinkle in Anse's eyes. Verl's face was growing wild, and Gilliam said, "Stop it, Verl. Can't you see he's just putting you on? Quit prodding him, Anse. I listened to him rave all the way back."

He shook his head at the offer of another cup of coffee. "I've got to be getting on to town." He stood and looked at Verl. "You're not damned fool enough to be thinking about going back there?"

Verl's grin was weak. "I've thought about it, but I'm not a damned fool. But I'll make no promises about what I'll do if I ever catch Captain Fear Not out of his county again."

Gilliam's grunt could have been approbation or disapproval. "I'll see you in town then."

Verl nodded and Gilliam left. Verl stood at a window and watched him as he rode away.

"I know Sam," Anse said. "Deep down something is chewing on him."

"The Mormons," Verl said shortly. "What are they drilling an army for?"

"You drill a militia company," Anse pointed out.

Verl started to argue there was a difference, and the argument had no solid basis. The Mormons had been run out of Jackson County. Perhaps they were determined it wouldn't happen again.

Anse wanted to erase the brooding from Verl's face. He said, "Will Rankin was by this morning. He wants to give us that pony he bought for the kid. It threw the boy and broke his arm. Will says his wife won't let him keep it on the place."

"What would we do with it?" Verl asked absently. A thought struck him and he swung from the window. "It's a fair-sized pony, isn't it?"

"About twelve hands. Why?"

"I was thinking of Blaine Phelps. It'd just about fit him."

Anse considered it then nodded. "It'd be a nice thing to do. It also gives you an excuse to go back there. What about Elly, Verl?"

Verl's eyes were dark with displeasure at the prying into his affairs. "Elly and I are good friends. There's never been anything more." It was all the explanation he intended giving.

Anse sighed. "If you know what you're doing—" he murmured.

Anse's words rang in Verl's mind as he led the pony. Rankin had been glad to be rid of it. It was a pinto with one moon eye. A moon-eyed pony could be pretty ornery, but Blaine should be old enough to handle it. He kept thinking of Anse's words–"If you know what you're doing," and admitted he didn't. He only knew there was a strong attraction for him at the Phelps' place, and it kept pulling at him. He thought irritably, Why worry about it? He was only repaying Blaine for possibly having saved his life. He didn't have to look beyond that now.

He rode up to the Phelps' house and yelled, "Hello."

He waited a moment then yelled again. He would feel like a fool if nobody was home.

Heather came to the door, and there was some kind of joy in her eyes as she looked at him. She was drying her hands on a towel, and she tossed it behind her. She hurried toward him, and her voice was a little breathless. "Father's not home. He went to town."

Verl said gravely, "I didn't come to see him."

That put a rosy flush in her cheeks.

He said, "I came to see Blaine. I've got something for him." He jerked his head at the pony.

She looked at the pony, and her eyes shone. "But you mustn't," she said in weak protest.

"Why not? I owe him something. Where is he?"

"He's cleaning out the barn. But—" She stopped and her face went still. Some uncertainty filled her eyes.

"Won't he like it?"

"He'll be tickled to death."

He thought she was going to refuse, then she called her brother. She said weakly, "I hope it's all right."

Verl thought, She's worried about her father. Phelps was a stiff-necked man and maybe proud enough to refuse a gift of any kind, even to a member of his family. If his guess was true, he'd have to work to change Phelps' mind.

Blaine came around the corner of the barn, and his face lighted at the sight of Verl. He bounded forward, and Verl grinned at him.

"I've got something for you, boy." He swung down and handed the pony's reins to Blaine and watched the awed rapture spread over his face. He was glad Rankin had thrown in the old saddle. The pony was all ready to go.

"For me?" Blaine said in disbelief.

"For you," Verl assured him. "Go on. Try him."

Blaine put his foot in the stirrup, and the pony danced.

Verl grabbed the animal's bridle and jerked on it. "He's a little high-spirited. Can you handle him?"

"I can handle him."

Blaine swung up and immediately had his hands full. The pony danced around in a wide circle, and Verl watched with a critical eye. The boy had a natural seat. But he had a few things to learn. Verl would have to come over here several times to give him instructions.

Blaine's face was a mixture of uneasiness and delight. He increased the diameter of the circle, and the pony picked up speed.

"Rein him in," Verl shouted. "Show him who's boss."

Blaine jerked on the left rein, and the pony veered so suddenly that he was almost unseated. A quick clutch at the horn saved him. The pony took advantage of the slack in the reins and bolted. It whipped around the corner of the house, and Blaine hung on for dear life.

Heather's face was worried. She didn't realize she clutched Verl's arm as she asked, "Will he be all right?"

"Sure," Verl said with more heartiness than he felt. He hoped Blaine could stick. This first ride was important in the amount of confidence it built.

He grew a little tense as the minutes raced by. And

the worried look was growing on Heather's face. He took her hand and said, "He's doing fine. He's giving him a good tryout."

She gave him a strained smile but made no attempt to free her hand.

The tenseness grew in Verl. What if Blaine had been thrown and hurt? Maybe it was time to go after him and see what had happened.

He checked his move as he heard the clop of hoofs. The sound grew louder, and Blaine rode around the corner of the house. He wore a big, cocky grin, and he held his head high.

The pony must have had a long gallop, for all desire to run seemed knocked out of it. Blaine kicked it into a faster pace and rode a wide circle around Verl and Heather. He stopped in front of them and jumped off. He threw his arms about the pony's neck and hugged it in an excess of feeling.

Heather tugged at her hand, and Verl realized he was still holding it. He let go and said, "See, didn't I tell you he'd be all right?" He felt limp with relief inside.

Blaine said, "He tried to throw me and couldn't. We're going to get along just fine."

"Good boy," Verl said, and the reflection of Blaine's grin was on his face. He looked at Heather and smiled, and she broke into that musical, tinkling laugh. The three of them shared in a warm, rich moment, bonding them together.

Verl asked, "What are you going to call him?"

"Gabriel," Blaine answered.

Verl looked startled. It was an odd name for a boy to pick for a horse.

He and Heather moved to the animal and both of them petted its neck. When their hands touched she didn't seem to mind.

None of them knew Phelps was near until he asked, "What's going on here?"

Verl turned, and Phelps' displeasure was in his voice and eyes. He glanced at Heather, and an uneasiness washed her face.

Only Blaine didn't catch his father's stiffness. He dropped the reins and rushed toward him, his eyes shining.

"Look what Verl gave me," he cried. He saw something in his father's face and changed it to, "Mr. Wakeman." The shining was beginning to fade from his eyes.

"We do not ask gifts of anyone," Phelps said.

Verl held his voice to a reasonable note. "It's no gift. It's a repayment of what Blaine did for me. It's little enough."

"No," Phelps said stubbornly.

"Father," Blaine cried. His voice broke off at the look Phelps gave him. He blinked hard as though he fought back tears.

"You and Heather go in the house," Phelps ordered. "I will talk to Mr. Wakeman."

Verl waited until the two were out of earshot. He must keep his control or he would push Phelps beyond reach of any words.

"You love your son, don't you?" he asked abruptly.

Phelps looked startled then nodded. "We are not questioning that," he said stiffly.

"Did you see the look on his face when you said no? He rode that pony, and it's a rough one for a boy to ride. It threw one kid and broke his arm."

Phelps' face remained obdurate, and Verl argued against it. "Your son accomplished something this afternoon. He grew a full foot."

The stiffness was fading from Phelps' attitude. He said uncertainly, "It is still a gift."

"It isn't. Don't you expect to pay for something done for you?" At Phelps' slow nod Verl said, "Then give me the same privilege. I owed Blaine that."

Phelps was silent, and Verl thought he had him on the defensive. "What's wrong with me?" he challenged.

Phelps looked startled. "Nothing," he muttered.

"You act like there is. All I'm asking is to be neighbors."

"It can never be," Phelps muttered.

"Why?"

Phelps stared at him, and there was a bleak, withdrawn quality in his eyes. "Because you are a Gentile. And I am a Mormon. We do not believe alike."

Verl managed to keep his shock from showing on his face. It was the first time he had ever been called a Gentile. The word had an odd impact.

Phelps said passionately, "I was driven out of Jackson County by your people. I saw our printing shop destroyed, our books burned. I saw one of our bishops tarred and feathered. I lost my property. Because I am a Mormon."

Verl thought of Heather and Blaine. There was nothing different about them. There was really nothing different about Phelps. They were just people like anybody else. He couldn't blame Phelps for his bitterness, but it wasn't fair to direct it at him.

He said, "I wasn't there."

Phelps' eyes widened as he caught Verl's meaning. "No," he said reluctantly. "But it is best that we do not mix."

"Why?" Verl asked again.

"Because our beliefs are different."

"Are they?" Verl asked. "You want to work your land, to prosper on it, to raise your family?"

"Yes."

"Don't you think I feel the same way?"

Phelps stared at him a long moment. "I guess you do," he admitted.

Verl smiled. "Then there's no reason we can't be neighbors?"

The long pause said Phelps was examining the idea from every angle. "I guess not," he finally said. He stuck out his hand, and there was a timidity to the movement.

Verl pressed the hand. It was the hand of a working man, it was a hand like his.

He didn't pressure Phelps about Blaine keeping the pony. He thought that permission was granted in the

66

handshake. He could see the joy shining in the kid's eyes.

He said, "I'd better be getting back to work. It catches up on a man mighty quick."

"It does that," Phelps agreed solemnly. He looked like a different man with the wary reserve melted from his face.

Verl walked to his horse and mounted. He was wise enough not to push farther today. He had a tiny foothold. The neighborliness could grow into friendship and there was no reason why it shouldn't.

He waved to Phelps as he rode past him and received an answering lift of the hand in return. He was whistling as he turned onto the main road. What happened in Far West and what happened here were two different things, and he kept them apart in his mind. He wondered why Phelps hadn't settled in Caldwell County with the other Mormons and was glad he hadn't.

Chapter Eight

Verl listened to Gilliam talk but his full attention wasn't on it. It had been four days since he had been to the Phelps' place. He wanted to go back. Every morning it was the first thing in his thoughts. But he wouldn't force the fragile relationship already established. Even though impatience pushed him the smartest thing he could do was to let things develop along normal, easy lines.

Gilliam said, "I've been nosing around the last few days. I guess I've kind of let things slide, hoping no trouble would come. But feeling is running pretty high against the Mormons. Ray County people hate them for taking part of their county, and there's plenty of feeling around here, too. A lot of Mormons have moved over into Daviees County. More than I realized."

Verl hid his guilty start. The Phelpses were a part of that "lot" that Gilliam spoke about. He guessed they had broken the law, for he knew of no vote letting Mormons take up land in this county. He thought, it's a bad law. A man should be allowed to take up any land that pleases him, if he can afford it.

"They're the damnedest people," Gilliam said. "They've got an organization called the Danites. The Mormons call the Danites the Destroying Angels. They go around catching and punishing people who have broken their law."

Verl gave him a grin. "Maybe over here we call it sheriff and deputy."

Gilliam looked annoyed. "I'll bet your Captain is one of those Danites."

Verl wouldn't doubt it. Captain Fear Not fitted the role.

"I don't care what they do over there," Gilliam said half angrily. "But they're not coming over here and following the same course. We've got an election in a couple of days. I'll need you."

Anse would scream when he heard of another day

off from work. Verl had ridden in today to bring the wagon home. Anse's fingers itched to get at that corn.

Verl had forgotten about the election. The voters would elect a new recorder of deeds and a tax collector.

"Why will you need me?"

"A family just moved out of Caldwell County. They came through here this morning. I talked to the man. He said it was getting too hot for Gentiles in Caldwell. He warned me that enough Mormons are in Daviees County to have an effect on the election. If they can put their people in it'll ease things for them."

Again Verl thought of Phelps and his family. Everything Gilliam said seemed aimed directly at them.

Gilliam's face was grim. "None of them had better try to vote in our election. Will you be here?"

Verl thought Gilliam was worrying unnecessarily. Still he had no valid reason to refuse him. "I'll be here," he said. He wondered what Phelps' reaction would be if he heard about it. Would he consider Verl's official presence a blow against him and all Mormons? He sighed inwardly. When men had different beliefs every move the other made was suspect.

"Keep it under your hat," Gilliam warned. "I'm not really expecting any trouble. I just want to keep on top of it before it crops up. If that damned Shelby hears about it he'll have his crazy Indians in town."

"Sure, Sam," Verl said and left. He stepped outside. Elly was coming up the street. He saw her eyes light up, and he felt uncomfortable. He wanted to speak to her, then move on, but she had no intention of letting him escape that easily.

"Verl," she said, and her delight at seeing him glowed in her quiet voice. "I just took a fresh batch of gingerbread out of the oven. I'll whip some cream."

His stomach accepted the invitation eagerly. He knew the gingerbread Elly baked. Spoon gobs of freshly whipped cream on it, and a man really had some eating.

He said lamely, "I haven't the time, Elly."

The light died in her eyes. "Not even fifteen minutes?"

Her reproach cut through to him, and he said gruffly, "Hell, Elly. I've got fifteen minutes."

"Don't put yourself out," she said. And now her tone was distinctly tart.

He grinned and took her arm. Elly was no doormat for anybody. "Come on. You've got my mouth watering."

He thought she was going to jerk free, then she was moving with him.

"You make me so mad," she said quietly.

"I affect everybody that way. It's a bad habit I've got." He felt guilty and disloyal and it made him irritable. He thought, I never said anything definite to her. There's no understanding between us.

As they passed the hardware store Shelby came out and joined them. His eyes gave him away. Every time he looked at her his eyes shone.

He said, "Elly, you get prettier every day."

Verl saw the color flowing into her face. He thought,

It's too bad she doesn't return Shelby's feeling. He erased the thought quickly. He wouldn't wish that on Elly.

Shelby asked, "What did you see Sam about?"

Verl drawled, "Grant, it's a wonder you've got all your nose left the way you poke it into things."

Shelby's eyes heated. "Dammit, I'm interested in what goes on in this town."

"Then go ask Gilliam."

It was hard to offend Shelby. He kept digging in like a tree-borer. "Is he worried about the Mormons?"

It was probably a lucky guess, but Verl said sharply, "What makes you ask that?"

"Because they're bound to cause trouble sooner or later. We're going to wind up by having to run them out of the country."

He was talking about Heather and her people, and Verl said angrily, "Get enough people talking like that and the trouble will come."

"Are you defending them, Verl?"

"I'm not defending anybody," Verl snapped.

They had reached Elly's yard, and Verl hoped she would invite Shelby in. It would give him an excuse to leave faster.

She said, "I'll see you later, Grant."

He gave her a hurt glance, then turned abruptly and stalked down the street.

"I've hurt his feelings," she sighed. "But he can be a pest."

Verl agreed whole-heartedly with that. He walked

into the kitchen, and the room was filled with a hot, spicy smell that brought saliva to his mouth.

She let him whip the cream. It was thick and yellow rich, and it didn't take many licks with the large spoon to build it into fluffy, white mounds.

He frowned at the portion she sat before him. "I can't eat all that."

She laughed. "You'll be asking for more." She had a good laugh, rich and easy. It transformed her face, softening the plainness. She sat across the table from him and picked at her gingerbread. "Verl, does Sam expect trouble?"

"You've been listening to Shelby too much."

"Don't treat me like a child, Verl. There's something on your mind, and I've seen Sam's face. And he's talking to everybody he can find."

"He always has. That's natural—" He saw he wasn't fooling her and stopped. "Yes, he's afraid of trouble. He thinks the Mormons might try to steal the election. I think he's wrong, but you know how Sam loves to worry." He remembered Gilliam's warning. "Elly, that's just for your ears."

She said passionately, "I wish every Mormon would leave. They're not like us. They don't want to be."

He scowled at her. "You sound like Shelby," he said harshly. "That's no good reason to hate them—because they're not like us." He pushed his plate back and got up. He walked to the door and didn't look back at her.

Chapter Nine

Anse leaned against the wall of McGinty's Tavern and watched the traffic move up and down Gallatin's main street. The election seemed to have brought out the families in the county.

He said, "Are we ever going to get started shucking that corn?"

"You didn't have to come in," Verl pointed out. "I promised Sam I'd be here." He saw the question in Anse's eyes and said testily, "No, he's not expecting trouble. It makes his office look more important to have a deputy with him." He hoped Anse swallowed that story.

Evidently Anse did, for he grinned. "I guess I came because I'm old and tired. I grab any excuse I can find to take off a day."

Verl thought, There isn't going to be anything to do except walk around town and look official. There might be a drunk or two to calm down and maybe a fist fight over a political argument. He could understand why so many people turned out for the election. Life on a farm could be drab and monotonous. A man seized any pretext to make a holiday, even to the point of riding miles to vote in an off-year election.

Anse said, "I'll buy you a drink."

Verl shook his head. "I have to look around."

He walked down the street, stopping here and there to exchange a few words with friends. He hadn't seen

Elly yet, and he hoped he wouldn't run into her. He owed her an apology for his abrupt departure the other day, and he was unwilling to make it.

He saw Gilliam standing on a corner, and hurried to catch him before he moved away.

"It's quiet enough, Sam."

"If it stays that way," Gilliam growled. "They're beginning to come into town, Verl."

Verl had seen quite a few families he didn't know. They had gathered in small groups, withdrawn from life in Gallatin. He had seen the hard looks given those families, and the bad feeling bounced off those stony faces. If they were Mormons, their presence here didn't necessarily mean trouble. Mormons had come into Gallatin for mundane reasons before.

Verl asked, "Do you think they came in to vote?"

"Cannaday says they won't. And he's the election judge. He won't let them vote until he checks out the length of residency in this county. And it's too late for that today. Keep an eye on the polling place, Verl."

Verl nodded and moved away. To his mind watching the saloons would be a better course. Trouble and drinking went hand in hand. But come to think of it he couldn't remember seeing a Mormon in a saloon.

The election was being held in a small building on a side street. A short-masted flag was tacked to the wall. Verl stepped inside. The election clerks sat at long tables, pencils and small squares of paper before them.

Ben Cannaday came toward him. He was a short man, heavy in the jowls and with an immense paunch.

He wouldn't be much good at a job of physical work or in a fight, but he was a fair-minded and determined man.

"How's the voting going, Ben?"

"Surprisingly light right now, Verl. I guess we'll get the rush in the afternoon."

"Any trouble?"

Cannaday shook his head. "I've turned away a half-dozen men. Neither me nor the clerks knew them."

"Mormons?"

Cannaday said dryly, "I didn't ask them. That wouldn't make any difference to me. If I know them and they've established the proper residency, they can vote. But none of them are slipping over here from Caldwell and having a say-so in our election."

Verl nodded. "I'll be around. Yell if you run into any trouble."

He turned and walked down the street. On the opposite corner some dozen men stared at him with impassive faces. It reminded him of the wooden stares he had received in Far West. If he had to he would say these men were Mormons. They announced themselves by their withdrawal. Cannaday's statement about Mormons coming over from Caldwell showed that he had it in mind. Surely none of the Mormons would be bold enough to vote illegally.

He passed the polling place several times in the next few hours. This parading around town was dull and monotonous. His stomach rumbled reminding him he had eaten a light breakfast. He stopped in Mrs.

Dundy's restaurant, and the place was crowded. She got to him finally and said, "I'm about out of everything, Verl. I never expected such crowds."

She was a slat-thin spinster with gray hair piled high on her head. Her church and her business were the only interests in her life, but she seemed content. Verl had never known her to say a hard word about anybody.

She said, "I've got a little roast pork left."

He nodded. "That'll do fine."

She served him and hovered over his table. She asked, "Verl, are the Mormons going to steal our election?"

A rumor had tremendous strides. It covered more ground than a man could believe possible. He managed a laugh and said, "I don't think so. Not with Ben Cannaday watching them."

She said passionately, "I wish they'd leave our state. They bring nothing but trouble."

He glanced at her in surprise. "I never expected to hear something like that from you."

"I don't care." The passion remained in her voice. "Their coming is changing the way we live, the way we think. And I don't like it."

The Mormon coming was a huge stone tossed into this placid pond, and the ensuing ripples washed everything in that pond. He admitted she was right about the change. It seemed to affect everybody in varying degrees.

Before he could answer her, he thought he heard a

shot. It seemed to come from the direction of the polling place.

Mrs. Dundy heard it too. She stared in that direction with a strained look on her face.

"Was that a shot, Verl?"

"Probably some drunk letting off steam," he said casually. He pushed back from his unfinished lunch, walked out of the restaurant, and quickened his stride as he reached the walk.

A crowd was packed before the door of the polls, and more people were running to join it.

"God damn it," Verl roared. "Let me through."

He fought his way to the door, and it wasn't much better inside. The place was jammed, except for a small, cleared space to the left of the door. Cannaday lay there, a red stain covering half his shirt front. A glance told Verl there was nothing he could do for him.

Ada Wilemette, one of the election clerks, stood over Cannaday, her mouth stretched wide with her screaming, her eyes glassy and dazed.

Verl reached her and grabbed her by the upper arms. "Stop that," he commanded. "You hear me?" He shook her, and the violence restored sanity to her eyes. The screaming subsided into faint whimperings.

"What happened here?" he demanded. He thought she was going back into the screaming, and the pressure of his fingers increased.

She closed her eyes briefly. When she reopened them they were clear. "Two men came in and wanted to vote. Mr. Cannaday challenged them. He ruled they couldn't vote. After an argument one of them drew a pistol and shot poor Mr. Cannaday." Her voice rose several pitches. "I was standing just this far from it all." Her hands measured a small distance. "They looked at me and I thought they were going to shoot me. Oh God! I'll never forget it."

Verl's head jerked around as he heard two more shots. They came from the northern edge of town. "Stay here, Ada," he ordered and plunged for the door.

He ran hard in the direction of the shots. He dreaded to hear more shots, and his mind and body were tensed against it. It had started and how far it would go depended upon him and Gilliam.

He saw a small crowd of people at the northern edge of town, and more people were streaming in that direction. He got just a glimpse of Gilliam before the crowd closed in again. Gilliam was squatting beside a man lying in the street.

He increased his pace and was panting by the time he reached the scene. Ed Parks was lying in the street. He had been shot through the head and chest.

Gilliam stood and glanced at Verl. His face looked grayer, more tired. "Two men did it, Verl. Billy Smith saw it."

Billy Smith was seventeen years old, man-sized but not yet man-experienced. His eyes rolled with excitement as he recounted his story.

"Two men came running down the street. Ed tried to stop them. Both of them were carrying pistols. They didn't even hesitate. They just shot Ed and ran on."

Verl supposed Gilliam had already asked the question, but he asked it anyway. "Did you know them, Billy?"

"They were Mormons," Billy said vigorously.

No Mormon wore a sign about his neck, yet Billy was positive about this much. Verl heard an angry rumble from the watching men.

"What was the other shot?" Gilliam asked. "I heard it but turned off when I heard these two."

"They shot Ben Cannaday. Probably the same two."

"They ran into the woods." Billy pointed to the timber two hundred yards away.

Verl and Gilliam headed toward the woods, and the crowd surged after them. The earth was still soft, and it took a good impression. The tracks they followed were spaced wide and planted deep, the tracks of running men. The running tracks ended where two horses had stood.

Gilliam said gloomily, "By the time we went back and got mounted up we'd never catch up with them." He glared at the crowd's howl of protest.

He looked at Verl and said, "We'd better go back and see about Ben." Something else was on his mind, and it put an urgency into his stride.

People were still packed before the polls, and Gilliam shoved against them. "Move, Goddamit," he roared.

Ada Wilemette was dabbing at her eyes with a handkerchief. "It was awful. Just awful," she said to anyone who would listen to her.

"Did you know the men?" Gilliam demanded.

She shook her head. "They looked like—" She hesitated.

"Say it."

She gulped and said, "Like Mormons. They wore beards, and their faces looked mean."

Verl thought, to a lot of people all Mormons looked mean. And maybe those two did look mean during the argument with Cannaday.

Gilliam yelled, "Anybody know them?"

A dozen voices raised in reply. "Mormons"

Verl saw Gilliam shake his head. That was no help at all.

Gilliam pulled Verl off to one side. Verl fretted at his deliberate manner. They should be after those two men.

Gilliam read the look on his face correctly. "While we're after them this town could explode. We've got a lot of Mormon families here today. In a couple of minutes we're going to have a riot on our hands."

He saw Verl's indecision and said, "Goddamit. Two eyewitnesses said they were Mormons. Do you think this town will need anything else?"

Verl nodded. Gilliam was right. "What do we do, Sam?"

"Round up as many of your company as you can. Arm them. Then patrol the streets. Move fast. Before this afternoon's through we could be counting bodies. I'll collect what men I can."

They separated at the door and ran in opposite directions. Verl rounded up Hoady and a dozen more men.

He told them what could happen, and Lycoming said, "Hell, I don't want to protect some damned Mormon."

Verl's eyes blazed at him. "Get out of here. You're no use to me."

Lycoming's face fell. "Aw, Verl. I didn't mean it that way. I'll do whatever you say."

Verl searched his face and was satisfied. "Come on, then."

He unlocked the company's armory and issued rifles. As he handed out the last one he heard wild yelling from down the street.

He said, "It's started," and raced down the street, the men pounding at his heels.

He pushed through a ring of howling watchers. Shelby had an old man down and was kicking at him. A half-dozen men from his own company danced around them, trying to get in a kick of their own. Not a spectator made a move to help the old man.

Verl grabbed Shelby's shoulder. He jerked him back and as Shelby whirled he slugged him on the chin. The blow knocked Shelby backward and dropped him in the dust. He pushed himself to a sitting position, his eyes groggy, but a fury beginning to spread over his face.

Verl stood over him with the rifle butt held at shoulder height, ready to bring it down in a crashing stroke. "Come on," he begged. "Try to get up. I'll knock your God damned head off."

The wild fury in his eyes lessened Shelby's intentions. "Jump him," he howled to his men.

"Shoot the first one of them that moves," Verl

ordered. Men shrank back before the ready rifle muzzles. Verl saw Britton slip hastily behind another man.

"You're protecting a Mormon," Shelby screamed. "A murderer."

"He didn't do it," Verl said shortly.

He helped the old man to his feet. The man bled at the nose and mouth, and his eyes were bewildered.

He said, "I am a Mormon. But I harmed no one. I only came to town to do my weekly shopping."

"You picked a bad day for it." Verl glanced at Hoady. "See that he gets safely out of town."

He watched Hoady and two others lead the old man away. He turned and faced a sea of angry faces. "Break it up."

They hooted at him, and he took a forward stride. "I won't tell you again." He took another step, and they retreated before him.

He looked at Shelby. "If I see you or any of your company even looking like trouble, I'll throw your asses in jail so fast you won't know what happened."

Shelby's face said he believed him. But the malignant shine in his eyes said, it isn't over.

Verl and his men patrolled the town. They broke up a dozen fist fights before the afternoon was over. Each time, he escorted a beaten Mormon out of town and saw him on his way. By late afternoon he was certain not a Mormon was left in town. Gallatin was beginning to calm, though men still gathered on corners, discussing angrily the day's affairs. He thought the moment of highest tension had passed, that now there would be only words instead of action.

Verl didn't realize until this moment how weary he was. He felt it in all his muscles. It was a deeper, more subtle reaction than that caused by physical labor. Most of this sprang from his divided sense of right and wrong, and it struck deep.

He thought he would make one more round of the town and if it seemed quiet enough he would call it a day.

He was passing through the east side of town when he saw the wagon approaching. Three people sat on the seat and even at this distance there was something familiar about them.

He stared at the wagon then broke into a run, his weariness completely forgotten. That was Heather, sitting between her father and brother.

A running man always denoted an urgency, and Phelps pulled the team to a halt. His face was tight when Verl reached him.

"What is it?" he asked and strain was in his voice.

Verl shook his head, trying to erase that strain. "I wouldn't go into town today."

"Why?" Phelps asked in a clipped voice.

"There's been a little trouble," Verl said reluctantly. "People still might be a shade upset."

He saw Phelps look at Heather, and there was a tragic shadow in both their eyes. Her lips trembled, and for a moment Verl thought she was going to cry. There was a shared remembering in that exchange of glances, and the remembering wasn't pleasant. Even Blaine's face was drawn, and some old specter of fear

83

haunted his eyes. He was old enough to remember too.

"Oh, father," she cried.

He patted her hand. "Don't," he said. His eyes were emotionless as he looked at Verl.

"Was the trouble between Mormon and Gentile?" he asked.

"Yes," Verl said honestly. "But it's stopped now. It's under control."

"It's never under control," Phelps said bitterly. His eyes were condemning.

Verl said with a flash of temper, "I've worked all afternoon trying to bring it under control. I've beaten up Gentiles because they were abusing Mormons."

It took a long moment for Phelps to reach his decision. "I believe you." His voice had softened. "But it will break out again, and each time it grows worse. But I thank you for the warning."

He hauled on the left rein, and the wagon made a turn to go back in the direction it came.

Verl watched it until it was almost out of sight. He thought Phelps appreciated the warning, and he was sure that had been a flash of gratitude in Heather's eyes. He sighed and turned back toward town.

Gilliam was standing at its edge, and he had seen the meeting. "Who was that?"

"A Mormon family I know," Verl said steadily. "I warned them not to come into town."

Gilliam's nod showed that the explanation satisfied him. He looked tired, and his shoulders drooped. Gilliam had known a busy afternoon too.

Verl's cheek hurt, and he raised a hand to it. He found a considerable swelling, and it surprised him. Sometime during the afternoon he had been hit and he hadn't even noticed it.

He said, "I think the town will simmer down. We stopped it before it got fully started."

"We didn't stop anything," Gilliam said gloomily. "We just saw it get off to a good start."

Verl stared at him. It was odd that Gilliam and Phelps said practically the same thing. And the two men couldn't be farther apart.

Chapter Ten

Gilliam looked tired as he dismounted before the Wakeman barn. The early twilight was chilly, and he shivered as the northwind got a bite at him. He nodded to Verl and Anse. "Would you feed a hungry man tonight?"

Anse was in high, good spirits. "We finally got started shucking today, Sam. Look at that corn. Why tonight I'd feed even you."

Verl finished unharnessing the team and led them into the barn. He measured oats into the manger and hung the harness on its pegs. He listened for a moment to the chomp, chomp as the animals began on the oats. He believed in heavy feeding if a man expected to get heavy work from a team.

He walked back out to the wagon, and Gilliam and Anse were discussing its heaped-up contents. At least Anse was. Gilliam was doing all the listening.

Anse held up an ear of corn that measured a foot long. "Did you ever see any better corn, Sam?"

"It's a fair-sized nubbin."

Anse laughed. "Nothing could make me mad tonight. Do you know Verl shucked and scooped a hundred and twenty bushels today? I don't even try to keep up with him any more."

Verl flexed his fingers to ease the stiffness in them. It had been a long day, and he felt the hours of it in his shoulders. He rolled them several times to ease them. He had been in the field since dawn, and he had never looked up. If a man intended to pick any corn he couldn't look up. He moved between two rows grabbing for an ear with each hand. He never looked for the wagon. That was a good team. They moved abreast of him neither drawing ahead nor lagging. The ears beat a constant drumming against the bang-board on the far side of the wagon and dropped into the bed. He tried to keep an ear in the air at all times, and the hard, monotonous work would go on for days. He was going to need a new pair of gloves in the morning. The rough corn husks were hell on cotton gloves.

Gilliam looked at the mud-caked wagon wheels. "Having trouble getting through?"

"In spots," Verl said. "It was frozen this morning. We broke through about noon." He kicked his foot to dislodge a piece of stubborn mud clinging to his boot. The stuff balled up on a man's feet until he collected pounds of it. Carrying the additional burden around added to the weight of weariness. A man never had any trouble sleeping during the shucking season.

"You and Anse go on in," Verl said. "I'll get this load off."

"Let it go until morning," Anse said.

Verl considered the temptation. But if he let it go tomorrow's work would be weighted with part of today's. The wagon was backed up to the crib. If he just made the effort of getting started he'd have it off before too long.

He shook his head. "It won't take me long."

He heard Anse and Gilliam talking as they moved toward the house. That is if he could call Gilliam's grunts conversation. Gilliam had less to say tonight than usual, and he wondered about that. He also wondered what Gilliam was doing out here this time of day. He sighed and picked up the scoop. At this rate it was going to take him all night.

The scoop's edge bit into the hard kernels of corn with a dry, snicking sound. He worked as methodically as a machine. His back bent, and his arms dipped and went forward. His arms rose as he straightened with a scoopful. Each scoop of corn clattered against the corn already in the crib and every now and then there was a cascading sound as the piled-up corn shifted to find a new level. He took one short breather before the wagon was empty.

He climbed wearily out of the wagon and walked toward the house; he was satisfied—he could make a clean start in the morning.

Before he entered the house he looked up at the sky. The stars glittered frostily. It was going to freeze again before midnight. Without a cover of clouds to hold the earth's escaping heat the temperature dropped early. He stepped inside the kitchen, and sniffed at the aroma of frying ham and potatoes.

Anse held an egg over the edge of the frying pan. "How many eggs do you want?"

"I'm too tired to care much."

"In that case I'd better make it three. It'll be ready by the time you wash up."

Verl poured water from the bucket into the tin basin. He was glad Anse or Gilliam had pumped a fresh bucket. He doused his face first then washed his hands. He dried his hands and face on the husk towel and walked to the door to throw the dirty water outside. There would be no more washing outdoors until spring.

He sat down at the table, and with the first bite his appetite came ravenously alive.

Anse watched him a moment then asked, "How'd you like to feed him when he wasn't too tired to eat?"

Gilliam shook his head. "It'd be a problem."

Verl grinned at them. His mouth was too full to talk.

None of them said much until the meal was finished. Gilliam belched comfortably. "Good meal, Anse." He extended his coffee cup for a refill.

Some worrisome thing was nibbling at Gilliam's mind. Verl said, "You didn't come out here to beg a meal, Sam. What is it?"

"Trouble," Gilliam said gloomily. "It didn't stop with election day. I'm getting a lot of reports from the Mormons claiming the Gentiles are raiding them and stealing their hogs and cattle. And the Gentiles are screaming the Mormons are doing worse. I rode my ass sore trying to check out some of the reports."

Anse said, "It'll blow over. You know how people exaggerate. A man loses an animal and immediately he screams it's been stolen. Saves him from looking for it."

Gilliam frowned. "This won't blow over. Everson got winged in the shoulder today. He claims he didn't see who shot him. I think he was trying to steal some Mormon's animals, and they got him. It's the damnedest thing how trouble brings out the thievery in men. Just give them the excuse, and they'll go raiding and looting. And scream to high heaven it's justified." He drank from his cup. "You never did learn how to make coffee, did you, Anse?"

Verl watched him with intent eyes. It always took Gilliam a long time to come to his point.

"A petition was circulated in Gallatin today," Gilliam said. "The damned thing looked like it was twelve feet long. It's already been through Livingston and Carroll Counties. People are fighting to sign it. They're petitioning Governor Boggs to drive the Mormons out of Missouri. You can bet on one thing. That petition is just the beginning."

"Then what?" Verl asked quietly.

"Then we'll have open war on our hands."

Anse looked incredulous. "No," he exploded.

"It's coming sure as hell. And Verl and me can't stop it. But we've got to try. But before it's over armies are going to be marching."

It took a moment for Gilliam's first remark to sink in. "What do you mean Verl and me?" Anse demanded.

"I've got to have him."

Anse banged the table with his fist. "Dammit! No! We've got corn in the field. We've got—"

"You may not have any place to put it," Gilliam said somberly. "You may ride in one night and find your house and barn burned."

Verl asked, "Anse, did you ever know Sam to go off half cocked?"

"No." Anse's belligerence was fading. He looked at his son. "Do you think he's right?"

"I think he could be right."

Anse's face was bitter. "I knew something like this would happen when you pinned on that badge."

"I won't go if you're against it."

"Hell yes you're going," Anse shouted. "You've got to go. How long?" he asked Gilliam.

"I wish I knew, Anse. I'm sorry. After Verl there's a big gap before I can come to another man I can depend on."

Anse couldn't hide the pleased glint in his eyes. "I can hire Plunkett to do a little shucking. Verl, give Sam all the time he needs. Take four or five days. Take a week."

Verl saw Gilliam start to speak and shook his head

at him. He knew what Gilliam had been going to say. This was big trouble. A week wasn't even going to scratch it. Anse was going to scream like a mating panther, but Verl would face that when he came to it.

"If you could ride in with me tonight," Gilliam said. He was asking a lot of a tired man. "Maybe you'd better plan on staying at the house for a few days."

That put pleasure in Anse's face. His thoughts were as plain as though he had shouted them. Verl would be spending a great deal of time around Elly. That would drive that new girl out of his head.

Verl held back sharp words. Let Anse think what he wanted to. He said, "I'll pick up a few clean clothes, Sam."

"I'll saddle for you."

Verl packed shirts, pants in a cloth bag. He put in his razor, strop and soap. If there was anything else he needed he couldn't think of it. He could always ride back out here after it. He wasn't going to the other side of the world.

Gilliam had the mare saddled when Verl walked outside. He tied the neck of the sack around the horn and mounted.

Anse looked up at him. "Don't take any talk from those Mormons. Break a few heads and they won't be so hard to handle."

Verl frowned at him. "You think they're responsible for all the trouble?"

"It wasn't here before they came."

That was the way Anse saw it, and there was no use

91

arguing with him. Verl said, "I'll keep in touch," and turned the mare.

He looked back after fifty yards. Anse was a lonely figure standing there.

Gilliam said, "A lot of people look at it the way Anse does. There's no more middleground now. You're on one side or the other."

Gilliam didn't mean it as a warning, and Verl didn't take it as such. Gilliam didn't know about the Phelpses.

"It's worse than you said, isn't it, Sam?"

Gilliam nodded. "I hear the Mormons have called out their Danites to protect their people." His smile was bleak. "You may run into your Captain sooner than you think."

Verl grunted. "The two of us won't be much against them." He wasn't arguing. It was just a statement of fact. He agreed with Gilliam. They had to try.

"Not a drop in the bucket. A lot of people are going to be hurt before this is over. You're going to see the militia called out."

That startled Verl. "Do you think so?"

"You wait and see. We'll keep what order we can until it happens."

Both men were occupied with their thoughts the remainder of the ride to Gallatin. Verl was concerned about the Phelpses. A lone Mormon family could be in danger. He would have to find a little time the next day or two and ride out and talk to Phelps. Not that he expected it would do much good. He was already familiar with that streak of stubbornness in Phelps.

The town loomed up ahead, and he heard the roar of a crowd and saw the bobbing light of torches.

"What's going on?" he asked.

"I expect anything now," Gilliam answered. He spurred his horse, and Verl followed him.

The crowd was before the general store, and Verl smelled the oily taint of kerosene from the torches. Shelby stood on the store's porch, and he was screaming something at the assembled men. After every sentence they roared passionately back at him.

Gilliam forced passage through the crowd with his horse.

"What's going on here?" he roared. In the wavering light his face looked tough and mean.

Verl waited on the edge, trying to take in all facets of the scene at once. Shelby had two dozen of his men with him. They were dressed in their Indian regalia, and three of them held fine horses. By the small, pointed ear and the sleekness of them Verl would say thoroughbred blood ran in their veins. Some of Shelby's men were drunk. They weaved as they stood, and their mouths hung slack.

Shelby turned a mocking face toward Gilliam. "We're tired of being overrun by the damned Mormons, Sam. We're tired of waiting for the law to do something about it."

The crowd bellowed approval, and Gilliam had to shout to quiet them.

"You'll do nothing," he said savagely. "You'll take nothing in your own hands."

Shelby held up his hands to quell the crowd's outbreak. "You want us to wait on you to protect us, Sam? You want us to let these damned cattle and horse thieves steal us blind? They've already taken our land. What have you done about that?"

"They've taken no land I know of," Gilliam said in an anger-congested voice.

"I wouldn't expect you to keep up with what's happening," Shelby said mockingly. "Do you know how many have settled in Daviees County right under your nose? The law says we've got a right to vote on whether or not they can settle in our county. Has there been any voting? But they're here. Nobody even knew they were Mormons until they took up their land." He grinned maliciously at Gilliam. "Our law didn't know. Our law didn't protect us. Those Mormons got their land by fraud, and that's the same as stealing."

He got roaring approval from his listeners, and it drowned out what Gilliam was trying to say. Shelby had scored some incisive points. Gilliam had lost the initiative, and he might not regain it.

Verl waited until the voices subsided then pushed his horse forward and stopped it with its muzzle almost touching Shelby's leg. "Look who's talking about stealing. Does it make a difference when our side does it?" He was sure an uneasy flicker touched Shelby's eyes.

"What are you trying to claim?" The bluster in Shelby's voice didn't ring quite true.

The crowd was silent. This was between two men,

and the intensity of the struggle showed in their faces.

"Where'd you get those horses?" Verl snapped. "I never saw them before." He looked at the crowd. "Any of you ever see them?"

The silence answered as loudly as though they had shouted, "No."

Verl said softly, "Grant, you and your Indians didn't steal them from some Mormon family, did you? If you didn't steal them you've got bills-of-sale to prove it."

The accusation jolted Shelby. His face showed it before he regained control of it. "That's a damned lie," he said hotly. "We were jumped by a Mormon band. We drove them off. They left the horses. We brought them in."

It was a thin story and poorly told. It buckled under the weighing of sober eyes. Only the men in Indian costume yelled affirmation of Shelby's words.

"You kept that information quite a while, Grant. Or weren't you going to mention it at all?" Verl's face showed savage delight at the hole he had backed Shelby into.

"Prove it," Shelby yelled.

"Why I don't think I have to," Verl drawled.

Gilliam took the crowd back. "Have you sunk so low that you approve of common thieving?" he thundered.

Eyes looked away from the hard impact of his. "I'll tell you this," Gilliam raged. "I'll arrest any of you for stealing. And I don't care if it's Mormon or Gentile. Now get on home."

His words smashed the solidity of the crowd. Men

muttered to each other. Then the crowd broke into little segments. The segments wavered uneasily and drifted away. Only Shelby and his men were left.

"Don't listen to him," Shelby yelled at the retreating men. "He's trying to protect the Mormons. He's—" He stopped as not a head turned. "God damn you, Sam," he said.

"What were you trying to do, Grant. Get them to ride with you against some other Mormon family? You haven't had enough raiding and stealing to satisfy you?"

"You can't prove a damned word," Shelby yelled.

"I wish I could," Gilliam said heavily. "If I get a complaint about those horses I'm coming after you."

The threat put no apprehension in Shelby's face. Verl thought, he's positive there'll be no complaint.

"I'm giving you thirty seconds to clear this street," Gilliam said. "Or I'll throw all of you into jail."

"What for?" Shelby sneered.

"For inciting to riot," Gilliam answered somberly. "And if you think I can't make it stick try me."

Shelby locked eyes with him for a brief moment. He stepped off the porch and said, "Come on, boys. That's the kind of law we've got protecting us."

They went down the street in a body, and their derisive remarks drifted back to the two men.

Verl said, "Sam, I wasn't trying to take over."

"It's a good thing you stepped in when you did. I'd lost them. Most of them are decent men. They're not quite ready to sink to outright stealing. But a few more abuses, and they'll do anything in retaliation and justify it. The Mormons will have men like Shelby. And between them they'll carry all of us into it."

"Do you think you'll get a complaint about those horses?"

Gilliam shook his head. "Mormons won't complain to our law. Even if these particular ones are alive to complain."

Verl wondered what lonely farm had been hit tonight by Shelby's company. If its occupants were alive would they consider themselves lucky to get off with only the loss of their horses?

He said fiercely, "I hope they make a charge."

Gilliam's voice was flat. "They won't. Lord, I'm tired. Let's get home and get some sleep."

Chapter Eleven

Verl awakened in the morning remembering the argument he and Elly had had the night before. She had insisted that the Mormons had started it, that there had been no trouble until they came. And that had been Elly of the gentle nature speaking.

He thought soberly as he dressed, it was easy to set people against people. One abuse begot another, and they snowballed into a giant crushing weight that was practically unstoppable. He had asked with dangerous quiet, "Because they believe differently than we do, are you saying it's all right to do anything to them? Even to murdering and stealing? If the Mormons feel the same as you do, they can come here. They can steal everything in this house and burn it down. If it's right for us it's right for them."

He had seen the catch in her breathing. That had put it on a different plane, that had made it personal. "You didn't have anything to do with the abuses, but you'd suffer just the same. Those Mormon women will be suffering too."

Her voice had been defensive. "You sound as though you're in complete sympathy with them." But the anger had gone from her face.

"He's tried to say he's in sympathy with law and order," Gilliam had said. "That's all. You two can argue all night. I'm going to bed."

That had broken up the argument. He wondered how she would react to him this morning.

He walked into the kitchen, and she was frying bacon. A bowl of batter was set beside a skillet.

"How many pancakes?" She kept her eyes averted.

He wanted this strain between them over with, and he said, "Elly, I'm sorry."

She faced him and shook her head. "I'm the one who's sorry. I'm so ashamed of myself. I thought only of Mormon men. I never thought of their women and children. I kept seeing them all last night. They're just as frightened as I am."

He wanted to hug her. He should have known that innate streak of honesty would come to the surface. "Maybe Sam and I can stop the fear before it spreads farther. You better make me about a dozen pancakes."

Her eyes sparkled at his forgiveness. "Only a dozen? Your appetite's puny this morning."

Gilliam came into the kitchen and saw the bantering in her face. "Good," he grunted. "You two reached an understanding."

Her face sobered. "Verl pointed out a few things I was too blind to see."

Verl felt guilt. He had pointed out those things because he knew and was interested in a Mormon family.

Elly put a stack of pancakes on Verl's plate, and Gilliam watched with amazed disbelief as they disappeared. "Elly, he can't help but wind up a fat, old man."

"Like you?" Verl asked and grinned.

"You just hope you wind up as good a man as I am." He had a frosty grin on his face.

He ate with indifference, and Verl knew he had a lot of weight on his mind. He asked, "How do we start, Sam?"

Gilliam said helplessly, "I don't know. I guess we'll wait until the complaints come in. If today's anything like yesterday we won't wait long. Why in the hell doesn't Boggs call out the militia? He's going to wait until it's too damned late."

He turned his head at the banging on the door; there was a tragic quality in his eyes. "We're not going to have to wait at all."

He strode to the door, opened it, and a half-dozen men stood outside. All of them tried to talk at once, and anger garbled their words.

"One at a time," Gilliam said. He pointed a finger. "You, Henshaw. What happened?"

"They burned out Cunningham last night. Stole every cow he had. All six of them."

"Who's they?"

"You know who I mean," Henshaw said furiously. "The Mormons."

"Did you see them?"

Henshaw's face darkened. "I knew you wouldn't try to do anything."

Gilliam's face turned violent. "You watch your mouth. We'll get out there right away. Maybe we can track them."

"That's not all," Henshaw yelled. "The damned Mormons tied Cunningham, his wife and two kids to trees. Then whipped them with hickory withes. They told them it was the Lord's punishment. They left them there most of the night in the cold. If we hadn't happened along they'd still be tied there. Those Mormons wouldn't have cared if Cunningham's family had froze to death or starved."

An uproar broke out from the men behind him, and Henshaw had to raise his voice to be heard. "I say we ought to hand out a little punishment ourselves."

Gilliam's eyes stabbed at him. "Against any Mormon family, Henshaw? Or against the ones who did it?"

The belligerent voices faded. They caught the difference, but their faces remained sullen.

"You can ride out with us," Gilliam said. "Come on, Verl."

A grim-faced cavalcade of men rode out to the Cunningham place. The neighbors were there trying to give what solace and comfort they could to Mrs. Cunningham. She was near hysteria, and she kept breaking into wails. Cunningham stood with stolid face looking at the ruins of his cabin. The ashes still smoked, and little plumes trailed lazily into the still, cold air. The eleven-year-old boy's lower lip trembled, but he tried to match his father's stoicism. Tears were streaming down the girl's face. She kept throwing her arms around her mother's neck and saying, "Don't cry, Mama. Don't cry."

Verl saw that the family had suffered more spiritual damage than physical. He wasn't minimizing it. That kind of damage left deeper, more lasting scars.

Mrs. Cunningham threw up her head, and her eyes had a blind intensity. "We weren't harming nobody. We were just trying to make a living." Her face twisted with ugly passion. "Kill them. Kill everyone of them," she screeched.

Cunningham looked at her. "You don't have to worry none about that, Sary."

Verl glanced at Gilliam. The tragic defeat had grown in his eyes.

Gilliam said, "Maybe we can overtake 'em, Ben. They won't be able to push those cows very fast."

Not a flicker of emotion showed in Cunningham's face. He said, "You won't." There was acceptance of his loss and contempt of the law's ability to relieve him in those two words.

"Any of the rest of you coming?" Gilliam asked.

They stared back at him with hostile faces. His expression showed he had a thousand things he wanted to say to them. He wanted to warn them, to plead with them, to reason with them, and not a thing would touch them.

He said abruptly, "Let's go, Verl," and wheeled his horse. He waited for Verl at the edge of the clearing. Verl joined him and looked back.

"They'll be hunting Mormons before night."

Gilliam swore helplessly. "It's like fighting a brush fire. You stomp it out in one place, and it flares up in another."

"We won't find those cows, Sam. They've had too much of a start."

"No," Gilliam agreed. "But we've got to try."

They cast a large circle and picked up cow tracks leading to the northeast. Horse tracks were so intermingled with cow prints that Verl couldn't tell how many riders there were. He looked at Gilliam and nodded. Both settled for a long, slow ride.

It was hard tracking for the chilled earth hadn't taken impressions too well. They worked their way along hardly making better progress than a cow's normal, shambling gait—and these cows were being pushed. They looked for prints in the frost on the ground, they looked for a scuffed place in the duff of the timber. They worked the miles steadily behind them, and a conviction grew in Verl's mind. They weren't going to catch up with those cows.

They stopped to let the horses water at a small stream, and Verl said, "Sun's strengthening, Sam."

Gilliam nodded. Soon even the frosty imprints would be gone then the tracking would be even slower. They would have only an occasional scar on the earth to guide them.

Gilliam lifted his reins. "Ready?"

Verl said, "Sure." Gilliam was a dogged man. He would keep on long after hope had faded.

Verl judged a good fifteen miles were behind them. He didn't know this part of the country very well. The hills and creek banks were wooded, but some of the bottomland was fairly open. They came out into a clearing, and a small log cabin was before them. Evidence of recent clearing was all around in the piled-up brush. A few pitiful acres had been broken and planted. It was slow, torturous work seizing land from the jealous forest.

"Know these people?" Gilliam asked.

Verl shook his head.

Gilliam said defensively, "And I'm supposed to keep up with everybody in the county. A family could live back in here for years, and I'd never know it."

"Sure, Sam," Verl said soothingly. "Let's go see who it is."

He thought the place had an unnatural stillness as they approached it. No sound of livestock broke it, not even the clucking of busy hens. He felt the tenseness creep through him. A farm place was never this quiet.

They came around the corner of a cabin, and a man

lay sprawled before it. He had been shot in the back, and the back of his coat was caked with dried blood.

Gilliam swung down and toed him over. Swarms of flies buzzed angrily. "Know him?"

Verl stared at the face and shook his head. The man was bearded. "A Mormon?" he guessed.

"You can bet on it," Gilliam said grimly. "Let's look inside."

There wasn't much in the cabin. The easily moved articles had been carried away. The rest had been smashed.

The shed was empty. "He had a horse and wagon, Sam." Verl pointed at the drying horse droppings and the marks of wheels where a wagon had stood. "If he had a family they've run."

"Or were driven off. We'd better bury him."

Verl started to protest that the family might be back for the body. But if they did come back they would discover the freshly turned mound.

He nodded. This family wasn't like the Cunninghams. They would have no friends or neighbors to turn to. They were aliens in a hostile land. If they returned it would be with reinforcements.

He said tersely, "Let's get at it."

He found a broken-handled shovel in the shed. Turning the earth with it was hard work. The silence had an eerie quality. He kept expecting it to be shattered with outraged cries, and it took effort to keep from scanning the woods.

He finished the grave and looked at its mound. It

was the best he could do. Gilliam's brush fire had broken out here. It would burn forward until it met the one started at the Cunninghams. When they met more people were going to be scorched.

"I guess that's it," he said and dropped the shovel.

He climbed on his horse knowing that the search for the stolen cows was dead.

Gilliam did too for he turned his horse toward town. He said savagely, "Will that God damned Boggs ever get off his fat ass?"

Verl understood. It was the protest of an overwhelmed man.

Chapter Twelve

Hoady met them at the edge of town; his face showed his excitement. Gilliam said wearily, "Look at him. Something else has happened."

"It sure has," Hoady answered. "General Atchinson is in town. He's been pacing a rut waiting for Verl to return."

"What's he want me for?"

"He's ordering your company out. He wants it ready to move by daylight."

"What for?"

"We're going after those Mormons," Hoady said soberly.

Gilliam said a soft oath, and Verl knew what was in his mind. If Boggs had acted this was wrong action, and it would throw the trouble into open warfare. Verl frowned at Hoady. He didn't see how Boggs had had time to act on a petition.

He asked sharply, "Where'd you get that?"

Hoady's face was solemn. "It's all over town. Shelby's been drilling his company the last couple of hours. They've been dragging that howitzer they've got every place they go."

Maybe that was envy in Hoady's voice. His company didn't have a howitzer.

"Where's Atchinson?" Gilliam asked.

"At your house. Elly's planning to feed him tonight."

"Good," Gilliam grunted. Maybe he could talk some sense into Atchinson. Maybe he could make him see that this move was unwise. He wanted the militia called out—yes. But not in a retaliatory move. He wanted them to help him police this county. For if militia from Daviees County rode against the Mormons, militia from Caldwell County would ride against Gentiles.

As they rode through town men called derisive comments at Gilliam. He was called a Mormon lover, and that was one of the gentle terms.

Verl saw his face stiffen, but his control was perfect. He didn't open his mouth.

Atchinson was in the kitchen finishing a second piece of Elly's deep-dish apple pie. Verl knew him from a previous meeting, and he stepped forward extending his hand.

Atchinson shook it then patted his paunch. "If I stayed around here long your woman would fatten me." He was a stocky figure with intense eyes in a bearded face. He was in field uniform, and his clothing and boots were travel-stained.

He asked, "Can your company be ready to march in the morning?"

"Yes sir. Under full arms?"

Atchinson nodded.

"How many men are you raising, General?" Gilliam asked.

"I want at least five hundred. I want a display of force that will make men think."

"Is your display of force ready to act?"

Atchinson frowned. "I'm afraid I don't understand you."

"Are you prepared to stop the burnings and stealings? Are you ready to run down the ones who did it regardless of who it was?"

"The militia is not a law-enforcement agency," Atchinson said stiffly.

"Then I'll tell you what you'll accomplish. You'll arouse the Mormons. That's all. You raise an army, and they'll raise one. And I'm betting they've got a better-trained one than yours. I've seen it. Are you prepared to fight them?"

Atchinson blinked. "My orders do not cover that."

Gilliam's face was incredulous. "My God, man. Do you think you're going to parade around the state and stop what's happening? I was hoping Boggs was prepared to act."

Atchinson's stiffness was more pronounced. "I think

you can trust the governor to know what he's doing."

Gilliam said contemptuously, "I doubt it. God, I need a drink." He turned and plunged out the door.

A scarlet cast was in Atchinson's face. "A completely unreasonable man."

Verl shook his head. "No sir. He's been carrying too big a load. He's been trying to keep people from killing each other. He was hoping your militia would stand between those people."

"You don't think a display of force will have a preventive effect?"

"No sir. Not unless you're prepared to use it impartially. I think Sam is right in his evaluation."

Atchinson's eyes were frosty. "An anti-Mormon crowd has gathered at Adam-on-Diamon. They'll disperse at my orders." He saw some stubbornness in Verl's face. "You don't believe that?"

"No sir. I think it's more likely that unless you're ready to use force to disperse them your militia will join them."

Atchinson sucked in his breath. The scarlet in his face was a deeper hue. "That'll be all, Captain."

"Yes sir." Verl walked outside. He swore softly as the realization hit him. The general had dismissed him from his own quarters.

He found Gilliam in his office, and Gilliam had the familiar water glass filled with whisky in his hand.

"I thought you'd have that down by now," Verl said.

Gilliam snorted. "This is my second one. That strutting little jay."

Verl said soberly, "Sam, he's got his orders."

"What are his orders?" Gilliam sneered.

"To disperse the crowd gathered at Adam-on-Diamon before they march on the Mormons."

"And if they don't listen to him?"

Verl shrugged. "He can't use force."

Gilliam swore until he was out of breath. "All he's going to do is to tear the lid off. I wish I had his men."

"How would you handle it?"

"I'd escort every Mormon out of Daviees County, then patrol the border between it and Caldwell. Then if they wanted an open war they could have it." He finished the glass of whisky without taking it from his lips.

Gilliam's way might be right, Verl thought. It would be brutal, direct action, but it might save a lot of lives. He wouldn't want to see it happen for one reason. The reason's name was Heather Phelps.

A whoop from the street turned his head.

"Shelby's collecting his Indians," Gilliam said. "Captain, you'd better gather your company. The general won't like to be kept waiting."

Verl ignored the thrust. "What are you going to do?"

Gilliam refilled his glass. "Why I'm going to sit here and get drunk."

Atchinson had camped his force outside town, and they marched in the morning. Verl's and Shelby's companies swelled the number of men to over three hundred. Other companies would join them enroute running the total to around five hundred men. The display of force was useless for it was a paper army unable to use the arms it carried. Shelby's Indians brought up the rear. Two of his men dragged the howitzer. Verl, riding near Atchinson, saw him wince each time Shelby's company whooped.

They marched up the Grand River, and they made good time. They camped out the first night on Splawn's Ridge east of Gallatin, and Atchinson used the old blockhouse as his headquarters. Every few minutes Shelby's Amaraguns split the night with their yelling.

Verl squatted by a fire roasting a hindquarter of a rabbit. That yelling was getting on his nerves. He wondered what Atchinson thought of it.

Markey came up and squatted down beside him. Markey was the newest member of the company, a lank man with shifting eyes. He spat a stream of tobacco juice at the fire. Something was on his mind.

Verl offered him part of the roasted meat, but Markey shook his head. "I've et, Captain." He stared broodingly into the fire.

Verl ate the hindquarter. It was well-done on the outside. It got a little raw near the bone.

Markey blurted it out. "Captain, some of the boys say we're not going against the Mormons."

He made a question of it, and Verl said, "We're not. We're going to try to stop big trouble before it spreads."

"Who we marching against then?" Markey's eyes narrowed with suspicion. "Not against our own people?"

Verl tried to explain, and Markey refused to listen. "The boys aren't going to like this. Hell," he exploded, "the only reason I came along was the chance for a little loot."

"There'll be none of that," Verl snapped. "And you pass the word." He locked eyes with Markey. "I mean it."

"Maybe the next election we'll get us a captain who's got some sense."

He saw the savage glow in Verl's eyes and retreated out of the radius of the firelight.

Verl poked viciously at the coals. Hoady came up and took the stick from his hand. "You trying to put it out? I wanted some hot coffee."

Verl told him about Markey, and Hoady said, "That kind of talk's going through all the companies. The men think we're moving against the Mormons. Aren't we?"

"No." Verl explained the situation as Hoady poured the coffee. Hoady stared at his cup, and Verl said, "Say it."

Hoady said bluntly, "I don't think the general can control them. They won't like going against their own people."

Verl kept his patience. "We're not going against our own people. We're trying to stop them from going against the Mormons."

"Same thing."

"I'll whip the first man who gets out of line," Verl said hotly.

Hoady grinned. "Does that go for me too?"

"For you too."

Hoady's grin broadened. "I believe you. I'll tell them. But I don't think it'll stick."

Verl sat for a long time staring into the fire after Hoady left. His anger fed on his helplessness, and it was poor fare. He wondered if other captains were having the same problem of control. Shelby wouldn't, he thought. Shelby believed as the rank and file.

They marched into Adam-on-Diamon the following night. The main street was packed with horses and wagons, and a tide of men flowed toward its far end. Verl could hear shouting there.

Hoady, riding beside him, said, "Something's going on. Did you notice that all of these men are armed?"

Verl had noticed something else. There wasn't a woman or child in sight. This was no pleasure gathering.

Somebody in the street yelled, "The militia's here. They've come to help us." The words were taken up. They swelled into a welcoming roar. By the light of a torch Verl saw the pleased look on Atchinson's face.

Verl thought, he's completely misjudged the temper of this crowd. Wait until they find out what he's here for.

The men in the street crowded around the militia until they could scarcely move. Verl heard the cry, "The militia! The militia!" repeated over and over, and there was a savage joy in it.

A sandy-haired speaker was standing on a hastily

knocked-together platform at the end of the street. He broke off talking at sight of the slow-moving mass and waited.

He bounded off the platform as Atchinson reached it and helped him dismount. "I'm Sanders. Welcome, General. We're glad you're here. Now we can move in force. We can drive every damned Mormon back into Caldwell."

Atchinson's face went pinched. Verl thought, maybe for the first time he realizes what he's up against.

The speaker helped Atchinson up onto the stand. "Say a few words, General."

Atchinson held up his hands until the crowd quieted. "We didn't come here to start war against the Mormons."

For a moment there was a stunned silence then a voice yelled, "I did."

It came from behind Verl, and he was sure it was one of the militiamen, maybe one of his own company.

The crowd hooted and yelled at Atchinson, and it took several minutes to regain quiet.

Sanders looked up at him and asked, "If you didn't come here to join us did you come to stop us?"

Hoots and catcalls grew in volume at Atchinson. A lot of the militia voices swelled them.

Atchinson was a rock under the abuse. He stood holding up his hands, his face patient. When he got a lull he cried, "I came to ask you not to take independent action. Governor Boggs will do everything necessary—"

His words were drowned under the indignant barrage of voices. Governor Boggs was chopped to pieces by angry words, and Atchinson came in for his share of it.

Sanders finally restored order. When he got his quiet he turned on Atchinson, and his face was fierce. "Three burnings this week and a man killed." He called out into the crowd. "Ives, how many cows did you lose?"

Ives yelled: "Nine."

Another voice yelled, "They stole my horses," and another claimed, "They took every damned hog I had."

Sanders faced Atchinson and said bitterly, "You hear that, General. Are you trying to make it easier for them?"

The voice of the crowd was as fierce as a prairie fire, and it scorched Atchinson. He tried desperately to make himself heard.

Verl caught fragments of his shouted words. "If you'll wait—Governor Boggs will—I promise—"

He gave up and stood helplessly, his face heavy with defeat.

Sanders let the crowd shout itself out. He was in complete charge, and his contempt for Atchinson showed in his face and voice. Atchinson either had no power to act or was afraid to.

"General, if you didn't come to join us or to stop us why did you bring an army? You could have come alone and accomplished as much as you have. Now get out of our way."

Verl saw the flare of temper in Atchinson's face and waited tensely. It was late for Atchinson to decide to stop them now. The militia was caught up in the tide of raw, unleashed passions, and Verl was afraid that only a small percentage of it would follow the general. At the moment he'd hate to vouch for his entire company.

The temper faded from Atchinson's face. He was under orders, and he would not exceed them.

Sanders said, "We knew we'd have to do it ourselves."

Atchinson climbed down from the platform. Not a hand was extended to help him. The crowd parted to give him a narrow lane, and Atchinson moved down it. As he reached Verl he stopped and looked up into his face. He was stripped of authority, and his face was heavy with defeat.

He said, "Captain, bivouac your company then report to me."

Verl picked a site well out of town. Sullen discontent was in the men's faces as they made camp. Raw excitement was surging in town, and they wanted to be a part of it.

Hoady made his report. "Twelve men missing, Verl."

Verl snapped, "Find them."

Hoady looked toward town. "In that mob?"

Verl said wearily, "Forget it." He knew how impossible the order was. "I guess I'd better see the general."

As he approached Atchinson's tent he heard an angry voice. Atchinson yelled, "Captain, you find those men and get them back to camp. I'm holding you responsible for their behavior. Do you understand me?"

"Yes, sir." The voice didn't sound too alarmed.

"That's all," Atchinson snapped.

The tent flaps parted, and Shelby's grinning face appeared in the entrance. The grin disappeared as he saw Verl.

Verl passed him without speaking. He stepped inside the tent, and Atchinson's face was furious.

"Captain, are all your men accounted for?"

"No, sir."

Atchinson said bitterly, "Can't any of you captains control your companies? The last captain here reports eighty per cent of his company is missing."

Verl was weary of this man. He took no advice, and he acted without knowledge of the situation. He had brought five hundred volunteers to an unpopular cause, and now he was outraged that the men were slipping away.

Verl said softly, "No more than you can control them, sir." It was rank insubordination and Verl knew it. He braced himself for the deserved explosion.

Atchinson chewed on his lower lip. An unconscious, pleading note was in his voice. "My orders extended only so far. Can't you see—"

He clamped his lips abruptly together as he saw not the slightest encouragement in Verl's face.

He said in a heavy voice, "I'm disbanding the militia. Take your company home in the morning, Captain. I've got to report to the governor on this new turn of events."

Verl said woodenly, "Yes, sir," and left the tent. He looked back, and the candlelight silhouetted Atchinson's figure against the canvas. The figure moved a few feet one way then retraced its path. Verl thought Atchinson was having a lonely, bitter look at himself. He hoped the picture sickened the general.

Hoady was staring moodily into a fire when Verl returned. "Some more men slipped away. I've given up trying to keep track of them." He stirred the fire and asked in a casual tone, "What did the general want?"

"He's disbanding the militia and sending everybody home."

"I figured he would," Hoady said moodily. "He didn't accomplish very much, did he?"

"Why he accomplished a lot," Verl said in an anger-tight voice. But it all had been on the negative side. "He showed the people they could not depend on the militia. Also that they need have no fear of it. He reinforced the ones ready to march on the Mormons. And he gave the Mormons an excuse to call out their own militia. What more could you want?"

Hoady clutched his arm. "Look!" He pointed toward the north.

Verl had already seen it, the orange glow on the dark

horizon that grew steadily larger and changed to a deep, crimson hue.

He said, "There's two more of them to the east." Three families were losing their houses and barns to the torch. It didn't make much difference whether they were Mormon or Gentile families. The night-riding terror had hit each equally as hard.

"What do we do?" Hoady asked in a small voice.

"Nothing. Just sit here and watch." Verl felt utterly weary. There would be many more of those burnings. And men would watch with equally helpless feelings. It would go on that way until somebody big enough and bold enough took hold of things and directed a united action. Then maybe the terror would be stomped out. That man wasn't going to be General Atchinson, Verl thought with a sudden surge of bitterness.

Chapter Thirteen

Twenty-one men rode back toward Gallatin with Verl. He spent no time looking for the remainder. As he mounted he said to Hoady, "If they've been doing a little raiding I hope the Mormons catch them."

Hoady shook his head without replying.

In the morning's ride they passed two farm sites that had been burned out. They found no bodies. Either the families had been warned in time to flee, or they had been allowed to go unharmed.

Verl looked somberly at the wreckage of men's

hopes and hard work. The ashes of the last place were still warm and smoking. An odd thought struck him. Looking at these ruins nobody could tell if Mormon or Gentile lived here. It was a grim fact that the only common meeting ground was in destruction.

He felt a compelling urgency to get back home. Anse was by himself, and the Phelpses were a lone family. He thought of Heather going through this terror, and he wanted to spur his horse. He didn't worry about Gilliam and Elly. They were in town with the protection of numbers.

He started to move the company and Hoady said, "A wagon coming."

Verl heard the rumble of its wheels. Perhaps it was the family who had lived here coming back to claim whatever they could salvage.

The wagon came around a bend in the road. A man and woman were on the seat, and the bed was packed with household possessions and kids. The man's face went ashen at the sight of the horsemen, and the woman's face was tragic with shock. The man stood and sawed on the left rein trying to turn the team. The animals responded slowly. By their appearance a night's hard travel had jaded them.

"Hold it," Verl called. "We mean you no harm."

The man sank limply back on the seat as though relief had melted his bones.

"You're not Mormons?" he said weakly.

Verl shook his head and heard the woman's sobbing.

She had ridden all night in the grip of fear, and the sudden release from its hold was too much.

"Stop it, Becky," the man said sharply. "We're all right." He looked at the ashes of a home and said, "I expect mine looks like that now. But maybe we're lucky."

"Did the Mormons drive you out?" Verl asked.

"I left while the leaving was good. We packed up what we could and drove all night. I came from Caldwell County. Any non-Mormon family living there now is crazy."

"What's happening there?"

"They're getting ready for war. I saw fifty men ride by our place yesterday afternoon. I'm telling you, Mister, I was scared they'd stop. Then I heard their Colonel Hinkle had called out every able-bodied man in Far West. That was enough for me."

"Which way were those fifty men headed?"

"This way."

Verl resisted the impulse to turn his head and sweep the surrounding country. Those fifty men had had ample time to ride into Daviees County. He wished he knew where they were.

"Do you want an escort?" he asked.

The man shook his head. "We're going to Adam-on-Diamon. We'll be all right now."

The kids whooped and hollered, and the man said, "You kids shut up." He gave Verl a faint grin. "Nothing ever wears them out."

Verl watched the wagon until it was out of sight.

Hoady said simply, "I guess it's started."

Yes, Verl thought grimly. It's started. Atchinson had raised the militia, and the Mormons had retaliated. Atchinson had disbanded his militia, but what was going to stop the Mormons? It had started out as a small thing, an abuse here and another there. But the abused had lashed back indiscriminately, and their actions were repeated by other men until it had swelled into monstrous proportions.

"What do you think?" Hoady asked.

"I think we'd better get back as soon as we can."

He forced the horses, and they made excellent time. By driving on into the night they could arrive at Gallatin after midnight. Verl considered it, then decided against it. Men and animals were weary. A night's rest and they could ride into Gallatin fresh in the morning.

He made camp near the banks of the river, and his nerves were jumpy. He debated upon ordering no fires, but that would cause grumbling for the men were cold. He knew the question that would be thrown at him. Where was the danger? He felt it was out there in the blackness, but he couldn't point it out.

He went from cooking fire to cooking fire ordering, "Keep it small. And put it out the minute you're through." He got some rough joshing about his fears, and his face grew more tense under it. Even in the timber a fire could be seen for a long way.

He posted two sentries, and that was really an unpopular order. Both men said, "Damn it, Verl. We're tired."

"You could be dead by morning," Verl snapped.

He prowled the camp long after the men were asleep, and a thousand doubts picked at him. Had he picked the best site he could? What other precautions could he take?

The sentries were on their feet and moving, but it was listless movement. Other considerations than danger were on their minds. The night's cold was baring its teeth and biting at them, and the thought of warm blankets was pulling them. He tried to prod them into alertness, but his words had no effect. The sentries would change at midnight. He hoped the next pair was more watchful than these two.

He walked down to the river and stared somberly at the water. It looked black and uninviting. His doubts grew. He had picked a bad spot. The river cut off one avenue of retreat, and the timber made good cover for attackers to slip up on them. He swore at himself. What was he doing even thinking of retreat?

Hoady found him and said, "You're fretting yourself to pieces. You'd better get some sleep."

"There's fifty Mormons out there someplace."

Hoady grinned. "Can you smell them?"

Verl said seriously, "It's a feeling I can't get rid of."

Hoady yawned. "Well you sit up and wait for them. I'm hitting my blankets."

The small, chilly hours of the morning were the longest Verl ever knew. He dozed off somewhere before dawn, and when he awakened the blackness of the sky had changed to a gray cast, and the first lighter streaks of dawn were in the eastern sky. He didn't know what had awakened him. It certainly wasn't because he had enough sleep for his eyes felt sticky and swollen. Some instinct had crawled over him, and it was the prickling of his skin that had snapped him into wakefulness.

He sat up and stared all about him. He neither saw nor heard anything unusual, and the snores of sleeping men were a normal sound. He didn't accept those things, for the early morning had a quiet, waiting quality that clawed at him with ominous fingers. He reached out and pulled his rifle closer to him. His eyes became accustomed to the poor light; tree trunks changed from the menacing figures of men back into their normal shape.

He stood and shook his head. A man's strained nerves could play him the wildest of tricks. He would go check the sentries then come back and start a fire. When the fire was going well he would arouse the camp for he wanted an early start.

He started to take a step and froze. He saw movement out among the trees, and it was furtive movement like a shadow slipping from one trunk to another. Only this shadow was garbed in white. And other shadows moved behind him.

Verl didn't know what had happened to that sentry out there, but there would be no further warning. He bawled, "They're here," and threw up his rifle and snapped off a hasty shot.

He heard a voice roar, "The sword of the Lord and

Gideon. Charge, Danites, charge." The voice had an oddly familiar ring, but he had no time to think about it.

All the furtiveness was gone from the movement coming at him. The woods were alive with men bounding at the camp. He fired an aimed shot and saw one of the attackers throw up his arms and spin before he dropped. The rest never even broke stride. They came at the camp in a fan, flanking it from both ends. And they were against bewildered, sleep-confused men. Some of Verl's men grabbed wildly for their weapons, others stood and watched in shocked stupefaction, and a few tried to flee. In their fear-induced blindness they fled straight into the attacking force, and Verl saw the flash of light against the flailing blades of swords. He heard one of his men scream, a high-pitched wailing that tightened a man's skin and tore at his guts. The screaming seemed to last forever then it stopped abruptly.

He had no time for an organized defense. The attacking wave was at the perimeter of the camp, and in a few seconds it would roll over them. He glanced hastily about and saw Hoady on his feet.

"Hoady," he bellowed. "Follow me."

He ran for the river and without breaking stride plunged into its chilly waters. His foot slipped on the muddy bottom, and for an instant he thought he was going to lose balance and go under. He gasped as the water soaked him to the waist and leaned forward throwing out his free hand to steady himself. The muddy bottom and the depth of the water made hard going, and his lungs burned with exertion before he was halfway across. He heard sullen hisses, and little geysers of water sprouted around him. For a moment he couldn't identify the sound or the cause of the geysers. It came to him with a frantic suddenness. They were shooting at him, and he felt nakedly helpless and vulnerable. His back muscles were tensed in anticipation of the slamming impact of a bullet.

He stumbled out on the other side and ran up the sloping bank. He saw the dead trunk of a windfall and threw himself behind it. He gasped for air to ease his tortured lungs. He heard the angry whacking of bullets against the log, and he pressed tighter against the earth behind it.

The fire in his lungs eased, and the red haze before his eyes lessened. He raised his head for a cautious look; Hoady had followed him. He was in the middle of the river struggling forward against the water's pressure.

A man stood at the far side taking deliberate aim at Hoady's back. Verl had no time to aim. He fired by instinct, and the light was good enough for him to see shock stamp the man's face. He stood upright for a long moment then teetered slowly forward. He fell with his face in the water and didn't move.

"Over here," Verl called, and Hoady staggered up the bank. He threw himself across the log and lay there gasping for breath. His eyes were fastened on Verl's face, and there was accusation in them.

The instant he found enough breath he said, "My God, Verl. You ran. And I followed you."

"You damned idiot," Verl snarled at him. He aimed carefully and picked off another Mormon who was hacking at a figure on the ground. Between breaths he said, "Maybe we can give them enough covering fire to let some of them get organized."

Hoady's eyes lighted. "You can knock me down later." He lifted his voice and bellowed, "We're over here, you bastards. Come and get us."

He aimed and fired, and a Mormon's running stride buckled and pitched him to the ground.

Verl saw some of his men running for the deeper woods. Some of them might get away, but too many figures lay motionless. He felt a sickness in his stomach and a cold rage in his mind. He had a bill to present for this attack, and each Mormon who fell was only partial payment.

The Mormons tried to get to Verl and Hoady. The white garbed man kept roaring, "Charge, Danites, charge." His waving sword pointed across the river.

Verl recognized that voice. It belonged to Captain Fear Not, and his hating choked him. The Mormon was dressed in an overcoat made of some white, blanketlike material, and he led the first charge down the river bank.

He had courage, Verl admitted. He was in the van all the way. Verl drew a careful aim on him and pulled the trigger just at the moment the Mormon's feet went out from under him. The fall saved his life. The bullet must have passed very close to him for he turned a startled face across the river.

Verl aimed again, but another Mormon got in front of his captain. Verl dropped him and looked for the man he wanted. But the fall had cost him ground, and now he was behind the others.

A dozen men started that attack, and Verl and Hoady broke it up before they were halfway across the river. Eight men turned and splashed back up the bank, running in wild flight. Four bodies bobbed in the slight current of the river.

"That'll make the bastards think," Hoady grunted.

"They'll come again," Verl said. His hands were busy reloading. The rifle barrel was warm to the touch.

Sporadic fire came from the timber, and Verl saw Mormons turn startled faces that way. A few shots came from the other side of the camp, and Verl's hopes grew. If his remaining men knew the same consuming anger, he knew that fire would strengthen. The rout had been stopped—at least temporarily.

Hoady said, "Here they come again."

Captain Fear Not was a brave but reckless man. He threw his remaining men into the charge across the river. They came in a yelling mass, and their first stride carried them far into the river. Their very eagerness was a handicap, for the footing was slippery, and some of them lost their balance and went under. They came up without their arms and were helpless under the withering fire Verl and Hoady poured into them.

Their courage carried them to the middle of the stream before they broke. Their forward momentum was stopped when a few made a backward step. Those first few steps became a rout, and men poured out of the water and up the opposite bank. Captain Fear Not led a charmed life for twice Verl fired at him. The man was close enough on the last one that Verl was certain he saw a sleeve of the overcoat twitch. He cursed himself for his eagerness and centered his sights on the man's back. The Captain changed course suddenly and ducked behind a tree before Verl could fire again.

For a moment there was silence; and after the yelling and hammering echo of gunfire, it hurt the ears more than the noise did. The river seemed filled with bobbing bodies, and the water had changed its color.

"That ought to stop them," Hoady said.

"I hope so." Verl held out his hand. He had five bullets in it. "That's it."

Hoady whistled and checked his supply. He shook his head. "I've got eight."

They stared at each other, and each knew what the other was thinking. If the Mormons made one more determined charge they would drive it home.

The crossfire from the woods was more sustained, and the Mormons buckled under it. The first, hesitant steps became a panic, and they broke and ran. Captain Fear Not screamed at them to come back, and not a man turned. He threw a final look across the river, and even from this distance Verl could see the hating in it. Then he ran after his fleeing men.

"I guess that does it," Hoady said. He stood looking for a final shot, but the Mormons were among the trees and offered poor targets. "No use wasting a bullet." He looked at Verl, and there was admiration in his eyes.

Verl leaned against the log. His eyes were dull, and he was limp with exhaustion. He felt the clammy grip of his sodden trousers send its chill stealing upward through his body. In the heat of the fight he hadn't noticed it before.

Hoady shouted in sudden elation, "By God, we beat them! We made the bastards run!"

Verl shook his head. One look at those still figures on the opposite bank drove all the elation out of him. "We paid a hell of a price for it."

Hoady looked across the river, and his face sobered. "It could have been worse. You saved us."

Verl assailed himself with self-blame. He hadn't saved them; he had led them into this trap. This was the first battle for the company. It was a far different matter than leading the company in a parade.

He waded across the river, and his heart was sick as he looked at the dead faces of men he had known for years. Some of them had been killed while trying to run. It looked as though a couple had been chopped down before they got on their feet, for they were still entangled in their blankets. Two of the bodies were horribly hacked.

A gleaming blade lay near a dead Mormon, and Hoady picked it up and tested its edge with his thumb.

"The sonsuvbitches used corn knives for swords," he growled. "You could shave with this." He tossed the blade from him.

Verl knew he had six men dead. He could count those. He didn't know what had happened in the timber.

Men filtered out of the woods, and some of the awful weight eased from Verl's heart at the sight of each one. One of them said, "Jules got his throat cut."

Jules was Verl's sentry on that side of the camp, and he had grumbled the loudest about the duty. Twice during his tour Verl had rebuked him for his indifference. Maybe Jules had dozed while some Mormon crept up on him. The camp had paid hard for Jules' lapse. Verl thought grimly, Jules had paid quite a price too.

He had seven men killed and eight wounded, two of them seriously. He sent two of the able-bodied men to watch for a possible return of the Mormons, and he thought he saw protest in Clevenger's face.

"If they come back," he said harshly, "nobody will be left to argue."

"I'm not arguing," Clevenger said hastily. "But they won't be back. I saw them running for their horses, and it was every man for himself."

Verl remembered that he had thought he heard the pound of retreating hoofs. Clevenger's words verified it. The Mormons probably wouldn't be back. He hadn't counted the Mormon dead, but he and Hoady had taken a fearful toll. And in the end the fire from the woods had cut down several of them.

"You keep your eyes open anyway," he said.

Clevenger and Lykins hurried off. There would be no indifference in them now, but it was a little late to be locking the door.

They gave what aid they could to the wounded, and Hoady and a couple of other men brought up the horses. By ordering the horses picketed deep in the woods Verl had saved them. It was a bleak consolation.

It was a sad procession that wended its way toward Gallatin. Seven men lay belly down on their saddles, and the wounded had to be supported as they rode. The miles fell behind them slowly and tortuously for Verl had to know that each bend ahead was clear, that no enemy was concealed in the timber before them.

He heard Hoady and the others congratulating themselves upon beating the Mormons. Verl couldn't feel that way. He was leading a decimated ccmpany back to Gallatin.

Clevenger rode beside him for a little way. "Quit blaming yourself. You saved us. I was running until you started pouring bullets into them from across the river."

The bitterness in Verl's eyes didn't lessen. He could have been prepared. If he had only done this or that— A thousand ifs paraded through his mind, and each left a scar.

"I'll tell you one thing," Clevenger said. "I'll shoot the next Mormon I see on sight."

A man had only to look at those limp forms dangling

across their saddles, to listen to the groans of the wounded, to understand Clevenger's words. Verl couldn't blame him at all.

Chapter Fourteen

It was almost dark by the time they reached Gallatin. He reined in suddenly as the town came into sight, and his upthrown arm halted the others behind him. The Murphys' house was a pile of charred rubble, and he could see three other burned-out houses beyond it.

He said in a strained voice, "They hit the town." Probably some time during last night. The Mormons had cut a fearful swath in a few hours.

"Stay here," he ordered. "Until I find out what's happened."

He rode on into town, and saw three other homes that had been burned. But the business district looked intact. The street was empty, and he could imagine people cowering behind their locked doors.

A man stepped out of a building a half block ahead, and Verl recognized Gilliam. "Sam," he called.

Gilliam turned and peered at him in the gathering darkness. "Is that you, Verl? My God, I'm glad you're back." He quickened his stride, and he was running by the time he reached Verl.

He answered the question on Verl's face with one bitter word. "Mormons. About ten o'clock. Almost everybody was asleep. It was your Captain Fear Not. With just about every man out with the milita we couldn't make a defense. They had us covered before we knew what was happening."

Gilliam's voice sounded as though he knew his full measure of self-blame too.

"They burned and sacked seven houses," Gilliam went on. "To show us Mormon vengeance was swift and deadly. Nobody slept much after they left. Some of the women are still wailing. We need your company now."

"I haven't got a company," Verl said harshly. He told Gilliam what had happened. Telling it brought it all back again. He finished and said, "I've got wounded, Sam."

"Everybody's down at the general store. Bring them there. I'll tell Elly and the other women to get things ready."

Willing hands helped the wounded men dismount. Verl saw a woman look at one of the bodies then break into frenzied screaming. Other women joined her as they discovered their dead. The town wouldn't sleep much tonight either.

They helped the wounded into the store. Elly had a pile of clean bandages, and she was tearing a bed sheet adding another to the ones already sacrificed. She went into a flurry of action when the first man was carried in.

Verl had no time to talk to her. She gave him a smile, but he noticed it was too tight around the lips. She must have gone through a bad time last night and throwing this at her wasn't any help. She took charge, and she kept the other women going. Verl watched her competent hands before he moved outside.

"You eaten?" Gilliam asked as Verl joined him. "I'll fry you some eggs."

Verl shook his head. "I've got to get out and see how Anse is."

"You can't. You're staggering now."

"It's blown wide open, Sam. A lot of people are going to get hurt. No family on either side is safe by themselves any more. I want to bring Anse to town."

He didn't tell Gilliam, but he had to warn the Phelpses too. A bitter thought scratched at him. Unless they already knew that Captain Fear Not and his company were trying to tear up Daviees County.

Gilliam took a deep breath. "Do you suppose this will make that damned Boggs act?"

Verl shook his head. He didn't know how Boggs would react, but he hoped he would send men different than Atchinson, men capable of handling whatever situation arose.

He walked to his horse, and his legs trembled with weariness. He mounted and lifted his hand to Gilliam.

Gilliam said gruffly, "You watch yourself, Verl."

Verl nodded and rode out of town.

He rode to the Phelps' place first; a single lamp was on in the house. Phelps was a foolish man leaving that light on as a beacon. After last night's events Gentiles would be marauding as ruthlessly as any Mormon band.

He hallooed the house before he came into the reach

134

of the lamplight. He called, "It's Verl Wakeman." He didn't want a nervous Phelps taking a shot at some unknown skulker in the darkness.

The door opened, and Phelps' figure was framed by the light behind him. He called, "What do you want?" and Verl detected strain in his voice.

He dismounted, and to his weary legs the steps to the porch were steep and endless. Phelps stood in the doorway blocking entrance. He evidently had no intention of asking Verl in.

Verl asked, "Is Heather all right?"

Phelps nodded. "All right." His tone carried no encouragement. Verl wasn't going to see her tonight.

"Did you know houses in Gallatin were sacked and burned last night?"

"I heard about it."

"The same band of men who did it jumped my company. A lot of men died. Do you know who they were?"

Phelps' mouth was a pinched line. "I suppose you people will blame it on the Mormons."

Verl noticed that "you people." An intangible but very stout wall had gone up between them. It was an effort to keep his voice calm. "It was Mormons. I identified them."

He was amazed at the rage he felt at this man because Phelps was a Mormon. He used more effort to keep his thoughts rational.

He said, "A family isn't safe by itself any more."

"You mean a Mormon family?" Phelps challenged.

Verl glared at him. "I'm not blaming you for what happened last night. I could. Your people started it. I'm advising you to leave with your family. Take them to Caldwell County."

Phelps' face was a stubborn mask. "This is my land. Nobody is going to run me off it."

Verl wanted to shout, You stubborn, old fool. He drew a deep breath. "You've got Heather and Blaine to think of."

"That's my concern." Phelps saw the rebuke in Verl's eyes and said passionately, "I have done nothing to anybody. I will not be driven from my land."

Verl said wearily, "Your business." If there were words to change this man he didn't know them. He walked to his horse and mounted. He stared a long moment at Phelps. The man's face was like flint.

He wheeled his horse and rode toward home. Short of picking up the Phelpses and carrying them away bodily he had done everything he could.

Anse was out in the yard when Verl rode up. "I heard your horse. I hoped it was you." He put out a hand and withdrew it hastily. He wanted to help Verl dismount, but that wouldn't do at all.

"You look beat," was all he said.

"I am." Verl walked beside his father to the kitchen. Anse wouldn't pry at him with questions, and he was grateful for that.

The kitchen was full of good smells, of boiling coffee and cooking beans. "I haven't eaten yet," Anse said. "I was figuring on frying some ham."

"I could use it." Verl was surprised at the ravenous reach of his hunger. This morning he could have sworn he would never know hunger again.

He didn't speak until he was satisfied. Anse always knew how to cook a pot of beans. He must have had these simmering for twenty-four hours at least.

Verl pushed back his empty plate and sighed. "That's better."

Anse took a deliberate time with the lighting of his pipe. "They hit Gallatin last night."

"I just left Sam."

"Do you know who led them?"

"I know," Verl said savagely. "I ran into him myself this morning."

Anse's eyes grew wider as Verl recounted the battle. The bitter self-blame was evident in Verl's voice.

Anse said reflectively, "I'd say you done real well."

Verl started to shake his head, and Anse said sharply, "Don't be a damned fool. You could've been wiped out. You didn't know the Mormons had hit the warpath."

"I did know," Verl said slowly. "But I didn't know where they were."

"You still did good."

Verl leaned across the table. "Anse, you've got to leave here. Go to Adam-on-Diamon for a while until this simmers down. It's a shooting war now. Neither side's going to stop to ask questions."

Anse considered it then asked quietly, "Aren't you going to be here?"

Verl shook his head. Maybe he and Gilliam could pick up a few more men, but there wasn't going to be a lot they could do. It was going to take a great deal of concentrated force to stop this thing now.

He said, "Anse, I can't." Anse's nod of understanding eased some of the distress in Verl's face. "I don't want you to stay here either. People in Gallatin are going to Adam-on-Diamon. It's bigger. The Mormons will think a second time before they attack it."

Anse snorted. "Not me. I got corn to get out."

"Dammit, Anse. It's not safe to stay here by yourself."

Anse raised his voice. "Don't you yell at me. I've lived here a lot of years, and nobody's going to run me away now."

Verl thought of another man he had talked to just a short while ago. Phelps felt the same way Anse did, and he expressed his sentiments with almost the same words. Yet they were enemies, standing on opposite sides.

Verl used all his logic trying to change Anse's mind. At times that could be almost impossible, and this was one of those times. Anse put a big boulder where his mind should be, and Verl couldn't budge it. The corn might wait, but Anse wouldn't. Didn't he have guns in the house? If Mormons came skulking around here he'd scorch a few of their asses, and they'd skedaddle in a hurry.

Verl wound up by losing his temper. "You hard-headed, old fool," he shouted.

"You watch your mouth," Anse growled. "You're not too big for me to whip."

A reluctant grin moved Verl's lips. Anse might not be able to whip him, but he would give it a hell of an effort.

He said softly, "Anse, watch out for yourself, will you?"

Anse's voice was gruff. "How do you think I got this old?" He saw the worry in Verl's eyes and said, "Besides I'll have somebody with me. Doc's coming out to spend a few days with me. I figure we're worth fifty Mormons apiece."

Verl laughed. "Maybe you are. I'd hate to have you two against me." The laughter didn't ring as true as it might.

Anse said, "I've got some cider that's turned pretty sharp. It might help us sleep."

Verl said, "I hope you've got a lot of it." Maybe the hard cider would help lessen the strains that pulled at him. He needed to be in a dozen places at once. The cider wouldn't put him in those places, but it could dull his thinking about them.

Chapter Fifteen

Verl looked at his father a long moment before he left in the morning. Words crowded onto his tongue, but there was really nothing to say that hadn't been said last night.

"See you, Anse." Verl rode off without looking back.

"Stubborn, old fool," he said aloud, but there was no anger. Instead the words held a deep fondness. Anse did what he had to. He had taught Verl the same lesson.

Gallatin looked like a deserted town when Verl rode into it. He didn't see a single person the whole length of the main street.

He dismounted before Gilliam's office, and Gilliam was inside. He stared broodingly at Verl before he spoke. "I thought you weren't coming back."

"I slept late. Where's everybody?"

"The able ones went to Adam-on-Diamon. Elly put up a fuss, but I made her go."

Verl's mind could rest on that score.

"A few hard-headed ones are going to stay," Gilliam went on. "They don't believe the Mormons will hit the same place twice. I thought Anse would be coming back with you."

"He's one of the hard-headed ones."

Gilliam clucked in sympathy. He hesitated a moment, and Verl knew he had bad news. "Stilwell died last night."

Verl had been afraid of that. Stilwell had been the most seriously wounded. "The rest of them?"

"They're coming along all right. Shelby came in right after you left last night. He was raving."

"About what?" Verl asked indifferently.

Malice was in Gilliam's faint smile. "He detailed part of his company to bring their howitzer back here. They were jumped by a bunch of Mormons near Millport. Shelby claims there were a couple of hundred of them. One of his men admits it was only a small bunch. Shelby's men ran. The Mormons got the howitzer."

Verl allowed himself a brief grin. "Where's Shelby now?"

"He rode out this morning swearing vengeance on every Mormon he could find."

Verl said sourly, "He ought to do well against a lone family. What happens now, Sam?"

He felt a bone-deep weariness. He couldn't muster enough men to stop Shelby. If Shelby was going up against the armed Mormons it would be a different matter. But he wouldn't do that. He'd hit the isolated families where there was practically no danger.

Gilliam scowled. "Boggs has to act now to put this down. But how soon? I guess the only thing we can do is to warn families to get out."

"On both sides?" Verl asked evenly.

"Both sides," Gilliam growled. "Did you think otherwise?"

"Then I'd like to ride out to the Phelpses. They're Mormons."

Gilliam's eyes asked a dozen questions, but he didn't comment. "I kinda thought they were. We can swing by their place."

He stood and said, "Lord, I'm tired."

Verl knew age didn't have anything to do with Gilliam's weariness. It came from a spiritual beating, and its effects were more draining and more lasting.

They passed three farmsteads, and each had a brooding silence about it. The families had fled before the mounting wave of terror.

"At least a few of them have got some sense," Gilliam said.

They made a wide swing and approached the Phelps' farm from the east. Verl asked suddenly, "Can we order anybody out?"

Again the questions were in Gilliam's eyes. "Nope. It's up to them. The law's got no power to drive a man from his home."

Verl thought, only the lawless could do that. Shelby and his Indians were roaming the countryside. Verl had to make Phelps listen to reason.

They came within sight of the house, and Verl hailed it. Only the echoes of his own voice rolled back. He tried again, and Gilliam said, "Looks like they're gone. We can check."

They rode into the farmyard, and a few chickens scratched busily about the barn. Verl walked up onto the porch and hammered on the door. An empty house always was surrounded by a feeling of loneliness, and he knew his knocking wouldn't be answered.

He came back and mounted. "They're gone. To Caldwell County I imagine."

He felt a relief and a sorrow. He wondered when and if he would see Heather again. But at least he wouldn't have to worry about her.

Gilliam asked a too-casual question: "He's got a pretty daughter, hasn't he?"

"Yes." Verl's eyes and tone had a brittle quality.

"Just asking." Gilliam swung his horse about. "We've got a lot of miles to travel."

Verl wished he could explain. Gilliam couldn't help but feel a degree of hostility because of Elly. Verl tried to sort out and put half sentences in order in his mind. They would all come out with the wrong note and only make matters worse. Both men rode in silence. A subtle gap had suddenly appeared between them, and Verl regretted it.

They covered many a mile during the day. They found a lot of deserted homes and some that were still occupied. They made the warnings as blunt and harsh as possible, but the stubborn ones just shook their heads. Verl saw the fear tighten their faces, but they still weren't leaving.

He asked helplessly as they left the last place, "What can you do with them?"

"Nothing," Gilliam answered flatly. "Each man believes it won't hit him. I hope they're right."

Their swing had carried them northward, and Verl said, "We're not too far from the Adam-on-Diamon road. We can cut through the timber ahead and find it."

Gilliam nodded. He rode slack-shouldered in the saddle, and weariness pulled at his face. "It'll be dark soon. I guess we've done all we could today."

The ground sloped upward where the timber ended. They threw startled looks at each other at the echoing crack of a rifle shot then sank spurs into their jaded mounts and galloped up the slope. They crested it, and the Adam-on-Diamon road lay before them.

A team and buggy careened wildly down the road, and a half-dozen men dressed as Indians were in pursuit of it. A man stood in the buggy lashing the team to greater effort. A woman and a boy were beside him, and the last of the day's sun struck red glints from the woman's hair. Rage choked Verl and distorted his voice. "You bastards," he yelled. He jerked his rifle from his scabbard.

It would be a long shot and a difficult one. He threw the butt to his shoulder and allowed for windage and the downhill drift of the bullet. He squeezed the trigger, and the shot must have been close for one of the horsemen ducked and sawed hard on his left rein spinning his horse around.

Verl kicked his horse into a full gallop and screamed curses at them. He heard the pound of hoofs behind him. Gilliam was following. Verl fired again and again as he drove toward them. The shots were fired in an excess of anger and from the unstable back of a galloping horse. He would be lucky if they came anywhere near. Still they had their effect. The horsemen were milling around, and the buggy was drawing away. He heard the slam of Gilliam's rifle, and he was close enough to see dismay flooding the horsemen's faces. He didn't think of the odds. All he wanted to do was to close with them.

One of the horsemen's nerves buckled under the menace of the determined, downhill charge. He whipped his mount about and plunged off the road cutting for timber to the southwest of him. That first break was infectious for the others followed. One man held for a moment and fired a shot at the receding buggy. Verl couldn't be sure, but he thought he saw Phelps reel.

He pulled up as he reached the road. The horsemen were scattering in wild flight. He might run one of them down, but he couldn't find and punish all of them. He raged at them until Gilliam reached him. Maybe Shelby wasn't one of them—at least he hadn't recognized him. But those were Shelby's men. He yelled a last wrathful remark and said, "Wait until I see Shelby."

Gilliam said dryly, "If you want to catch that buggy we'd better be at it."

Verl looked up the road. The buggy had used its advantage of the interruption to draw steadily away. If Verl couldn't make himself seen or heard it was going to take a long, hard chase to run the buggy down.

He asked a lot of a tired horse, but it responded. When he thought he was within earshot he yelled, "Hold up. It's Verl. Verl Wakeman."

Either his voice didn't carry, or complete panic had seized Phelps for the buggy didn't slow. Phelps still stood but he no longer flogged the team. One arm seemed to be hanging limp.

Verl swore and asked for more from his horse, and it slowly cut the gap. He yelled again, and this time he knew Phelps could hear him. "Pull up, Phelps. Pull up."

Phelps turned his head. He should have recognized Verl, but he made no effort to haul in the team. There was no doubt about his right arm hanging limp.

Verl looked angrily at him as he passed the buggy. He rode beside the off horse and, leaning far out of the saddle, missed the bridle with his first grab. He made it on a second try and felt the strain of pulling the team down run up his arm. The team didn't run far. It had been hard used, and it welcomed the chance to stop running.

He got them stopped, and they stood with drooping heads. Their breathing was hard and gusty, and foam flecked their muzzles.

Verl glared at Phelps. "What's the matter with you? You saw it was me."

Blaine said, "Paw, I told you it was Verl. I told you."

Phelps gave him a sharp look, and the boy subsided.

Phelps said, "I wasn't sure how you felt today."

Verl stared at him in outrage. Of the three only Blaine was glad to see him. Heather was crying, and she hadn't even looked at him. What did it take to prove friendship to these people?

Phelps saw the accusation in Verl's face. "Those were your people chasing us," he pointed out. "We have a right to any doubts."

"Dammit. It wasn't me." He'd driven Shelby's men off. What more proof did Phelps want of the way Verl felt. Heather's crying was intensifying, and Verl said sharply, "Stop it!" It was over. He was tired and wounded in spirit. He couldn't see she had any reason to be bawling now.

She looked at him wide-eyed, and tears sparkled in her eyes. But her crying lessened.

Gilliam pounded up, and he looked from Verl to the people in the buggy. His eyes came back to Verl, and Verl bristled at the weighing in them.

Phelps still stood, and he swayed. His mouth was a pinched line of pain. A spreading, red stain covered the upper arm of his coat.

"Get down," Verl said. "And let me look at that arm."

"It's nothing," Phelps protested. "We're not too far from Adam-on-Diamon. I have friends there."

Verl wanted to yell, What the hell did he think he was? He said, "Get down."

Phelps obeyed unwillingly. Verl examined the arm, and Phelps was wrong about the wound being nothing. The shot Shelby's man had fired had been a lucky hit. The bullet had passed cleanly through the upper arm leaving a nasty hole. Verl prodded and poked as gently as he could and still heard Phelps' sharp suck of breath. He decided no bones were broken, but he had to stop that bleeding.

He needed a longer strip of cloth than his handkerchief. He looked at Heather and said, "Give me your petticoat."

He saw the red wash her face and said impatiently, "Hurry." This was no time for her to turn finicky on him.

She dismounted on the far side and, keeping the buggy between them, removed the garment. It seemed it took her forever, and he wanted to shout against her false sense of modesty.

She came around the buggy and, keeping her face averted, handed him the petticoat.

He tore the garment into strips. The mouth of the wound was a raw, purplish-puckered hole. He wadded up a piece of the material and said, "Hold it there." He tied strips of cloth around the arm binding them tightly. The bleeding slowed, then stopped. If it took them too long to reach Adam-on-Diamon he would have to release the bandage.

Phelps looked at the bandage. "I'm grateful." There was still reluctance in his voice.

"Sure," Verl said ungraciously. A man had a right to expect more than he was getting.

"I mean it."

Heather hadn't said a word, and Verl felt no softening toward them. He scowled at Phelps. "What were you doing out here anyway?"

Phelps sighed. "After you left last night I thought I saw men skulking about my place. I sat up the entire night thinking of Heather and Blaine. I figured I should get them away."

Verl thought sourly, his figuring came a little late. "Why didn't you head for Caldwell County?"

"I tried," Phelps said simply. "I was cut off three times by bands of men ahead. I was afraid to find out who they were. Then I tried for Adam-on-Diamon.

Those men picked us up this afternoon. I hid in the woods and thought I'd escaped. But they wouldn't give up." A shudder ran through him. "They were gaining on us. I kept thinking of Heather—" His voice ran down.

Verl's feelings toward him softened. The fear had been enough to make any man suspicious. He could forgive all of them their reactions. The day had been a brutal club against them.

He said gruffly, "We'd better get on." He glanced at Gilliam.

All this time Gilliam had sat there without saying a word. That God damned weighing quality had increased in his eyes.

"Is that all right with you?" Verl shouted.

"All right with me," Gilliam said levelly. It wasn't a complete agreement. It left too many things unsaid and said too many things by implication. Gilliam's face had changed too. It looked older and grayer. Verl thought guiltily, Elly's on his mind, and his anger rose. He would not accept any blame or criticism in this. He had done nothing to merit it.

He stopped once on the way to town to loosen the bandage. The bleeding started again, but it was only a seeping instead of a flow. Phelps' face was drawn with the pain of the wound, but he didn't make a murmur.

It was getting dark when they entered Adam-on-Diamon. Verl wished he could find Elly. He needed her to check his doctoring. He asked Gilliam where he could look, and Gilliam gave him a long, deliberate appraisal. He thought Gilliam was going to refuse then he said, "You might try her cousin's house. I told her to go there." Again the unsaid things on his tongue hammered at Verl.

They stopped before the frame house at the edge of town. Verl felt a strange hesitancy. "Shouldn't you go ask her?"

Gilliam said roughly, "You go ask her. You want her to do it."

Verl walked up to the door and hesitated with his fist upraised. He looked back at the buggy. Phelps was sagging in the seat. He needed better attention than Verl had given him. Verl brought his knuckles savagely against the door. He hadn't intended to knock quite that hard.

Elly opened the door, and her face lighted at the sight of him. "Verl," she breathed. "I've been worried about you all day."

He was afraid she was going to fling herself on him, and he retreated a step. "I've got a wounded man out here, Elly. Will you look at him?"

"Sam?" Her breathing seemed to stop momentarily.

"He's all right."

Color returned to her face. "Bring him in. I'll get things ready."

"He's a Mormon, Elly."

She blushed from the remembrance of their prior conversation, but her voice was steady. "Does that make a difference?"

"No," he said. "I guess not."

He went back to the buggy, and Phelps protested at coming in. "I can find my friends," he said stiffly.

He insisted upon putting Verl in the opposite class, and it was hard for Verl to keep the anger out of his voice. "Maybe you can. There's been trouble around here. Your friends may have been run out. And you can't afford to spend time looking for them."

"Please, Father," Heather begged.

The pain and the weariness wilted Phelps' stubbornness. He murmured, "Maybe I'd better."

Verl and Sam helped him to the door, and Elly held it open. Her face warmed as she saw Gilliam. She gave him a brief hug then turned to Phelps. "Let me look at that wound."

Verl introduced her to Phelps, and she said, "Come in, come in." Heather stood in the shadows of the porch; Elly hadn't really seen her yet.

Introducing her to Elly was the hardest thing Verl ever did. "Elly, this is Heather. Heather Phelps."

Elly stared at her, and something died in her face. She looked at Verl then back at the girl. Verl thought miserably, she knows.

"Come in," Elly said again, but there was no life in her voice.

She led the way to the kitchen and sat Phelps on a chair. She removed the bandages, and her fingers were as competent as ever. But there was a great difference in her: she moved mechanically.

Verl stood out of the way and watched her. A misery gnawed at him. I should have told her. The

151

thought was like a hammer beating against his brain.

Elly talked to Gilliam as she worked. "Milly and Jim went to Millport." At Gilliam's frown she added, "But they'll be back in the morning. Jim's worried about his mother. He wants to bring her back here."

Gilliam said, "They shouldn't have left you alone here."

Elly shrugged with complete indifference. She poured hot water into a pan from the kettle on the stove. She washed the wound, and the bleeding didn't start again. She glanced once at Verl. "You did a good job." Her eyes were a million miles from him.

She cleansed the wound thoroughly then smeared a salve on it. Even with her gentleness Phelps winced. "It'll be sorer in the morning." She might not have meant it that way, but it sounded cold.

She turned to pick up fresh bandages and bumped into Heather. Heather had watched her wide-eyed and white-faced. She hadn't been much use.

Elly said, "Will you get out of my way?" It was sharply said; it was the only indication of the pain of her thoughts.

She finished the bandaging and adjusted a sling around Phelps' neck. "That'll take the weight off it."

Phelps started to rise. "It feels better. I'm grateful to you. We'll be going—"

She pushed him back into the chair. "You'll be going nowhere with that arm tonight. We can sleep you here. Milly won't mind."

The weakness forced Phelps to accept. He settled back and said, "I'd be grateful."

152

Verl wanted to yell at him for using that damned word again.

Elly bustled around the stove. "I'll fix something for supper."

Verl shook his head. "Not for me, Elly." He couldn't stay in this room another moment. Elly didn't look at him, but Gilliam did. And there was the same accusation in Elly's withheld eyes as there was in Gilliam's open judging.

He said, "I'll get the horses and buggy off the street."

He stopped outside and wiped his face. He wasn't surprised to find sweat on it. A man sweated under the kind of blame he had felt in that room.

He took a long time getting the horses unharnessed and settled in the shed. He found some oats and fed them. He would have to pay Milly's husband for those oats. He didn't want to go back into that house. He stood at the door of the shed wondering if he could sleep here. But if he did would it make things more obvious than they already were?

He didn't see Heather until she spoke to him. He jumped at the sound of her soft voice. She said, "Verl," and those enormous eyes searched his face.

He said, "Yes," and his heart was thumping hard.

"I haven't said thank you."

A warm smile spread over his face. "You don't have to."

"Yes I do. I should have done it before. But those men frightened me. Then I saw father shot." She sighed faintly. "I didn't stand up very well."

"You did just fine."

She looked toward the house. "Not against her. I didn't stand up well at all. Who is she, Verl?"

"A girl who lives in Gallatin." He didn't want to talk about Elly.

"Is she in love with you?"

Verl shrugged helplessly. "How do I know?"

"She is." Heather moved nearer. "Are you in love with her?"

"No." Maybe the word came out too violently, but he couldn't help it.

"I think I'm glad," she murmured.

Her face was upturned to his, and he was lost in the depth of her eyes. He felt power and fear at the same moment. There was a sweet singing in his veins as he reached out for her. She came into his arms, and there was just a little fear in her. Her lips quivered under his mouth, and he made the first contact gentle. Then her lips firmed, and she answered his demand.

The kiss could have lasted a second or an eternity. He lifted his head and stared in wonder at her. The fear was all gone, and only the power remained. He felt drunk with it. He had so much to say to her, and only her name came to his mind. "Heather," he said huskily, putting all the endearment he felt into the saying of it.

Her eyes searched his face, and the faint smile on her lips strengthened and grew. She raised a hand and moved her fingers along his jaw.

"When did you know?" he asked.

"I think when I first saw you."

He wanted to hear more, and the eagerness showed in his voice. "The very first time?"

Before she could answer a low, angry voice called her name.

She gasped and pushed away from him.

Verl saw the trembling in her before he turned to face Phelps. He felt anger at the interruption. If Phelps had the wrong idea about this he would put him straight in a moment.

"Go in the house, Heather."

Verl prayed she would disobey. He even raised an arm to put about her to give her strength.

She ducked under the arm and said weakly, "Yes, Father." She was gone before Verl could stop her.

He looked at Phelps and made no attempt to disguise the dislike in his eyes. "I'm not good enough for her?" he asked coldly.

Phelps shook his head, and there was stubbornness in the gesture. "It cannot be."

"Why can't it be?" It was hard to keep from shouting. "I love her. She feels the same about me. Because she's a Mormon, and I'm a Gentile—"

"It cannot be," Phelps said again.

Verl never realized before how much he disliked this man and his blind obstinance. "Tell me why," he said hotly.

"She is promised to another. To one of our own kind."

Promises of this sort had been broken before, and

Verl felt reassurance returning. "That doesn't matter now."

"It cannot be changed. She is promised to Mace Norton. She will marry him."

Verl remembered the man the Mormons called Captain Fear Not. In Far West a woman had called him Mace, a woman Verl was certain was married to him.

"Is that the one you call Captain Fear Not?"

Phelps nodded.

Verl felt like laughing with his relief. "But he's already married. I know—"

"That is part of our belief," Phelps said stiffly. "You will not see her again. I'm taking her to Far West in the morning."

He started to turn away, and Verl seized his shoulder. He dropped his hand at the wince of pain twisting Phelps' features. He had forgotten about the wound. Now his voice was raised, and he didn't care.

"She has something to say about that."

Phelps looked at him with cold eyes. "She has nothing to say." He turned, and this time Verl didn't stop him.

Anger and sickness warred within him as he watched Phelps walk back to the house. He examined that kiss again and again, and he knew the miracle of it would never leave him. It wasn't going to be as Phelps said. He wouldn't let it be. And Heather wouldn't let it be either. He built on that thought, but it didn't bring the comfort it should have.

He stayed outside until all the lights in the house

darkened except in the kitchen. One wild plan after another raced through his mind, and he discarded them all. He knew one thing for sure: he would see her again. And she would leave with him.

He walked to the house; Elly was in the kitchen. She looked at him, and he wished she would accuse him with her voice instead of just her eyes.

She said, "You'll sleep in the room there with Sam." She pointed to a door leading off the kitchen.

He knew she hadn't waited to tell him that. She started to turn away; his "Elly" stopped her.

He didn't miss the hope springing into her eyes. He had in mind to try and explain to her, but what could he say? He shook his head wearily.

She looked at him a long moment before she turned away. It was hard to watch hope die in her eyes.

Chapter Sixteen

Verl awakened at dawn after a sleepless night. During the night he had listened to Gilliam's soft snoring. He didn't hear it as he dressed. He wondered if Gilliam was awake. If so he hoped he didn't speak to him. He thought, A man made a decision, and it changed the whole course of his life. It cut him off from some people and made him feel closer to others.

He looked back at the door. The light was just strong enough for him to see Gilliam's form. He felt a queer wrench at the thought of not seeing him again. He had always felt close to Gilliam.

He stole across the kitchen floor and cursed its squeaky boards. Somehow he had to arouse Heather. He was quite positive that after last night she would listen to him. The problem was to get a few moments to talk to her.

He stepped outside and scowled at the blank windows in the rear of the house. He didn't even know which room she was in. He moved to the shed to saddle his horse. He wanted everything in readiness. He entered the shed, and a voice startled him. He whirled, and she was just inside the door pressed against the wall. Her eyes were hollowed, and the usual radiance in her face was missing. Heather had also known a bad night.

"Verl," she said. "I prayed you would come here."

He strode toward her, his arms extended. His face held a fierce joy. Phelps couldn't stop them. Nobody could.

She slid away from his touch and shook her head. "Don't. I have to talk to you."

He dropped his arms. "And I wanted to talk to you." His voice was forceful with confidence. "I'll get a horse for you. We can leave before anybody's up." He could borrow Gilliam's horse and send him payment for it later. Gilliam would cuss about it but do nothing more. He thought of Elly and abandoned the idea. Under the circumstances it would hardly be fair. It didn't weaken his confidence. He would find another horse for Heather.

"I don't need a horse, Verl. I'm not going with you."

He heard her, but he didn't believe her. He said hoarsely, "You've got to go, Heather. I'll take you any place you want to go." That caused him a sense of loss. His roots were buried deep in Missouri soil. But later, after all hostilities had faded away, they could return.

She shut her eyes, and he saw a tear roll down her cheek. But she was shaking her head. "No," she whispered. "I cannot go."

"Why?" he insisted. "You know I love you. Last night told you that. You love me. I know it."

He reached out and seized her arms. "Heather, look at me. Tell me you don't love me."

She gave him a flash of her eyes, and they were filmed by tears. "I think I do. I'm not sure," she gasped.

Hers were the normal fears of a young girl. His confidence returned, and he smiled at her. "You'll learn. It won't be hard."

Her eyes were closed again. "I cannot go."

He felt a terrible rage. He wanted to shake her, and he stifled the impulse. "Why can't you?"

"I cannot leave my father."

"Because he's wounded? He'll be all right. A couple of weeks and that arm will be as good as new."

What was the matter with her? He wanted to scream the question at her. She wasn't even listening to him.

"It's against my belief," she said faintly.

"I have a belief too," he said savagely. "I'll be giving up some things myself."

That was the wrong tack, for he saw a stiffness steal into her face.

"It isn't the same."

"Why isn't it?" His rising anger was pushing him along, and he couldn't stop. "Do you know what your belief's going to do to you? It's going to take you back to Far West so you can marry Mace Norton. Is that what you want?"

"No," she whispered.

"But you're going ahead anyway because your father wants it, because your belief demands it. Doesn't it matter what you want?"

Her silence gave him answer enough. They stood on opposite sides of a wide canyon, and their voices reached each other only faintly.

He felt a rage—at her, at everything. He said coldly, "Then why are you standing here? Why don't you hurry to Far West?"

Her sob didn't touch him. He wanted to hurt her as brutally as he had been hurt. "Did it all amuse you? Did you come out here to laugh at me?"

She sobbed again. "I wanted you to understand. I may never see you again."

"You chose it," he said harshly. "You'd better get back to the house before they miss you."

She searched his face, and she saw only the flint-hard exterior. She didn't see the terrible hurt he was trying to hide in his eyes.

She turned and plunged out of the door. She was running as she crossed the backyard.

He screamed at her to come back, but it was all inwardly. For if he had a dozen voices he couldn't turn her. She had come out here expecting his understanding to support her. Maybe he had failed her. But what about him? She hadn't given him a thing.

His eyes were blind as he saddled his horse. His fingers were stiff and fumbling, and he worked with a frantic urgency. All he wanted to do was to get out of here, to put as many miles as he could between this place and him.

He mounted and put the horse into a hard run. He forced it until it was blowing, and it wasn't the stiff, chilly wind that whipped tears into his eyes. He let the animal rest, and his face was slack. The raging fire of emotion had burned out leaving him listless and drained. He hadn't told Elly or Gilliam where he was going or even that he was leaving. It didn't matter.

He let the horse have a slower pace as he headed back toward Gallatin. He was going home, he was going back to the farm where he belonged. And nothing was going to pull him away from it again. Let the damned fools kill off each other. As long as they touched nothing of him he didn't care. And he and Anse would see that they weren't bothered.

He only thought he had the wild sense of loss under control. Every so often it would come sneaking back and attack him full force. He would remember the touch of her lips, the way she looked into his eyes, and again he would try to run away from it. It was hard on the horse, but it made for good time along the road.

161

He made a lonely camp, but sleep wouldn't take him. Staring into the fire was the worst thing he could do, for he kept seeing her face in the flames. He was on the road before dawn, and he suspected he looked like hell after two sleepless nights.

He steeled himself as he neared the farm. Nothing must show on his face. Anse mustn't suspect a thing. Verl wasn't afraid of his ridicule. No, Anse would try to use sympathetic words, and they would be heavy and awkward. But secretly, he would be glad. Everybody would come out of this feeling glad—except Verl. He wouldn't even credit Heather for feeling sorrow.

He stopped the horse as the farmhouse came into view. He leaned forward and patted its neck. "I'm sorry, lady. But you won't be going any place again for a long time."

He thought a last time of Heather. She should be well on her way to Far West by now. He would not allow himself to think of her again. And if his mind turned treacherous he would blot it out with hard work. He nodded as though he had discovered a great, new principle. Hard work was the answer.

Everything looked normal as he approached the house, but something made his skin tingle. This was a warm house. It shouted its welcome to anybody who approached it. But the warmth and welcome were gone, replaced by a brooding loneliness.

He saw the broken, front window, and a great cold seized him. But that was only the result of an accident.

In some way Anse had broken the window. He had gone to Gallatin to find replacement glass. That would explain the lonely atmosphere around here too.

Verl wanted to believe it. How desperately he wanted to believe it. His eyes remained fixed on the window, and he saw the ugly scars around it. Bullets would make such gouges in the wood.

He swung down with a hoarse cry and rushed into the house. Anse and Doc Courtney lay on the floor just under the window. The room was literally shot to pieces.

He couldn't think, and his muscles refused to move. He didn't know how long the shock held him in its iron grip. He finally managed to throw it off knowing he had to do something.

A glance told him Doc was dead for he lay on his back, and his sightless eyes stared at the ceiling. He had bled hard. His shirt front was a mass of blood.

Anse lay on his side his face turned from Verl. Verl was afraid to approach him. Afraid to confirm what he already knew.

He said in a choked voice, "Anse?"

"That you, Verl?" a feeble voice answered him. "I tried to hold on. I kept praying you'd come back."

Did he really hear a feeble voice, or was it just part of this horrible nightmare?

"Verl?" The voice sounded impatient.

Verl rushed forward and dropped to his knees. He turned Anse onto his back, and Anse groaned. "Easy, boy," he said.

His face was bloodless; his breathing a thin, reedy sound. He had been shot in the chest and had bled freely. It had taken tremendous vitality to hang on this long.

"You're going to be all right," Verl cried. That hole in Anse's chest belied the words.

Anse's attempt at a grin was ghastly. "I don't think so, boy. I guess the bastards stole everything they could carry away."

"Who was it, Anse?"

"The bearded Mormon who knocked you out in Hoady's place. He had a bunch with him. They came at us right after dawn."

His eyes closed, and Verl thought he had gone.

Anse opened his eyes. "Doc's dead?"

Verl nodded.

Anse tried to chuckle, and it put a racing cough in him.

Verl held him until the spasm passed. "Don't talk, Anse. I'll get someone to look—" His voice faded. Who could he get to doctor Anse?

"No use." Anse's voice was very faint. "How many times have I called Doc soft? He gave one hell of an account of himself." Pride was in that reedy voice. "We took some of them with us, Verl. We—"

The words stopped, and his head fell forward.

"Anse," Verl cried frantically. He couldn't call loud enough to reach Anse now.

He held his father for a long time, and he needed release from the bitter tears bottled up inside him.

He said, "Anse, I'll find him," and laid him back

down on the floor. He stood and walked to the door. He moved as though he were asleep, and his thoughts and motions were equally disjointed. He had to get a hold of himself. He had so much to do. He had to get Anse and Doc ready for burial. He had to build two coffins and dig the graves, and it would be a monstrous task for a lone man. But he had to do it. He knew Anse would want to be buried here. But what about Doc? He forced himself to think about it. Doc had no family. Verl guessed that if Doc could say he would pick to remain with his old friend.

The tears came as he worked on the coffins. They blinded him and dripped onto his hands until he couldn't see the tools.

Gilliam said from the door of the barn: "You made good time. Elly said she saw you ride off. I left soon after. I never caught sight of you."

Verl looked at him. He didn't try to stop the tears; he wasn't ashamed of them. "They killed Anse," he said chokingly.

"I know. I looked in the house before I came out here. You'd better let me give you a hand with that."

His matter-of-factness steadied Verl. They worked in silence. Gilliam would have to guess at Verl's gratitude. He couldn't express it.

Verl didn't speak until the graves were ready to be filled. "Sam, if you could say something—"

Gilliam looked helpless, then he said, "Lord, these were good men. They did their jobs the best they could." He showed emotion for the first time. His face twisted, and the words wouldn't come. He tilted a fierce face toward the sky. "Goddamit. Why?"

He looked at Verl and shook his head. "I'm sorry, Verl."

He needn't be. It was as good a preaching as Verl had heard at a funeral.

They filled the graves, and Verl turned and walked toward the house. No more fumbling thoughts raced through his head. He knew what he had to do.

Gilliam caught up with him, and Verl said, "It was Mace Norton." The name would mean nothing to Gilliam, and Verl added, "Captain Fear Not. I'm going after him."

"Even into Far West?"

"Even any place," Verl said flatly.

"How'd you like some company?"

Verl shook his head. He was grateful for Gilliam's offer of help, but this was something he had to do alone.

"A lot of help. I stopped by the office before I came out here. I had a message from Boggs. He's finally acted. I guess all those petitions were enough to scare any politician. He's ordered the Mormon regiment in Caldwell to be disarmed and disbanded. He wants the leaders arrested and all other Mormons to be expelled from the state. He's ordered out all the Missouri militia to go to Far West to carry it out. I'd say you're going to have about two thousand men with you when you go in."

Verl stared blankly out across the countryside, and

Gilliam asked patiently, "Did you hear me? You're going to lead your company, aren't you?"

"I'm going to lead it."

"Good. You got a vacancy in your company an old man could fill?"

"A good man," Verl corrected. "There's one thing, Sam. Norton's my business."

Gilliam's voice was soft. "Why I'd never think of poking in a man's private business."

Chapter Seventeen

It was almost noon before Phelps could leave Adam-on-Diamon. Elly had insisted on redoctoring his arm, and she had protested it was foolish to be traveling with his wound. But he was in a Gentile household, and they were equally as uncomfortable around him as he was around them. He had insisted upon walking downtown to buy food to replenish what his family had eaten, and his stubbornness had overwhelmed their arguments. While in the store he had heard the alarm news. The Missouri militia was marching against Far West. The Mormons might already know about it, but he had to carry the news to them.

He kept the team moving at a brisk pace. Heather sat beside him, and her face was wan. He said a half-dozen times, "It is for the best, child."

She hadn't answered him yet, and he smothered his rising irritation. She would get over it. Time was all she needed.

He said, "We must pick up your aunt at Haun's Mill. She will be fussy about moving." His sister could be difficult, and she detested moving. But he would feel better if all of his family were in Far West. Only twenty Mormon families lived at Haun's Mill. It wasn't sufficient number to offer any kind of protection.

He drove to the mill late in the afternoon. Jacob Haun had built well on the north bank of Shoal Creek. The blacksmith shop was of sturdy logs although in need of chinking. Some of the gaps between logs were an inch or better in width. But that would be taken care of later when there was time to be turned from the building of homes. A half-dozen houses were already constructed, but more were needed to take families out of tents and covered wagons.

The late afternoon sun had little warmth, and he shivered. It wasn't altogether due to the chilliness. The little hamlet looked so pitifully undermanned.

He stopped before Emily's house. Her man had been industrious, but he had been a sick man before the house was finished. He hadn't lived long in it. Yes, Emily would fight against leaving.

His sister was a woman of ample girth. Perhaps that was why no one had asked her to marry again. But she had a pleasant face and a disposition to match. He waited patiently until the greetings were over, until the huggings and exclamations of pleasure had weakened.

Emily wiped a tear from her eye. "I didn't expect a visit from you."

Phelps' face was somber. "It's not a visit, Emily. They are moving against us again."

Emily's face went tragic. She had been in the exodus from Independence, and she wouldn't believe it could happen again.

"But they promised—" she started.

"Who can believe a Gentile's promise?" Phelps said bitterly. "I want you to come to Far West. You'll be safer there." At the protest forming in her face he said, "You will come. It would be wiser if everybody here moved."

Emily weakened under her brother's authority, but a spark of defiance remained. "I will not leave without my things."

"Lord, Emily, I can't take all that junk in my buggy." He knew his sister. She would want to take every movable item.

She said angrily, "Who's asking you? I have my own wagon. I've agreed to move. But I'm not abandoning my things. Please. I'll be ready to leave in the morning."

He didn't want to refuse her, but he had to push on to Far West. A night's delay could make a tragic difference.

"I can't stay."

"Heather and Blaine can stay with me," she pleaded. "They can help me pack. We'll be ready to leave the first thing in the morning."

It wasn't wise, but he relented. They would only be a few hours behind him. "I have your promise?" At her nod he said, "I'll expect you in Far West by noon,"

He hugged Blaine and kissed Heather's cheek. For a moment he thought she was going to turn her face from him. As he walked away he heard Emily say to Heather, "What's wrong with you, child? You look peaked."

Phelps had to warn the people here before he left, and he found a half-dozen men in the blacksmith shop. His news put two of the older men in a panic. One of them dropped to his knees and prayed the Lord to send his angels to help them.

David Evans shouted, "Stop that. We've got nothing to fear. We've got enough men to drive off every Gentile who comes up against us."

Phelps knew Evans as a Danite, and as such he had authority. He looked at him with troubled eyes. "How many men can you raise? Thirty?" He saw the flicker in Evans' eyes and knew he was near the correct number. "And what kind of arms do you have? Shotguns and squirrel rifles?" Again he saw that flicker. "The Gentiles will be better armed."

Evans' face darkened. "Are you saying I don't know what I'm doing?"

Phelps said obstinately, "I'm saying you're responsible for a lot of people." He pointed to a body of timber and brush just north of the mill. "If they get in there they will be on you before you know it."

Faces looked out of the door, following his pointing.

Beyond the timber was a wide stretch of open prairie. Phelps said, "At least keep a picket in the north edge of the timber. He can see them coming for a long way. You'll have time to make preparations."

Heads bobbed at the sagacity of his warning. The black rage remained on Evans' face. "I'll take care of the mill. You get about your business."

Phelps stared at him soberly. He had warned him. He could do no more. He turned and walked out of the shop. He wished he could take back his promise to Emily. He wished all of them were going with him right now.

The wagon was piled high with household goods. Heather shivered in the chill morning air. She despaired, feeling that her aunt would never stop bringing more things from the house. She said, "Aunt Emily, we can't take any more."

Emily looked at the packed wagon and nodded reluctantly. "There are some other things I'd like to take. I guess I'll have to leave them."

Blaine was the man of the group, and the importance of it made him walk inches taller. He inspected the wagon's running gear and said, "Aunt Emily, the right rear rim's loose. We'll lose it before we go a mile."

Emily sighed with exasperation. "Then we'll have to stop at the blacksmith's and get Jacob to hammer it back on."

An old man answered her pounding on the shop's door. She said, "Jacob, will you knock a loose rim back on?"

He gave her a sour look. "Before breakfast?" he grumbled. But he walked into the shop then came back with a jack and a sledge hammer. He raised the wheel and pounded on the rim. Between blows he grunted, "Won't stay long without soaking. How far you going?"

"Far West," Emily replied.

His face went still. "I think all of us should go. But Evans won't hear of it. He's got everybody crazy. Even the women are yelling, 'stand firm.' They're offering to mold bullets and get patching ready for the rifles. I hope he knows—" The remainder of his words were drowned by a burst of rifle fire. A man walking across the street dropped as though he were clubbed. A yelling, screaming horde of Indians burst out of the timber.

Haun had a stunned, disbelieving look on his face. "Why damn him. He didn't even put out a picket like he was warned."

Women and children cried and screamed in terror. The woods grew right up to the edge of the hamlet and there was no time for organization. A dozen people directed by a few men ran across the mill dam to the south bank of the creek and sought shelter in the woods to the south of the creek.

Haun squinted at the dam and said, "Too far. We can't make it." He shoved at Emily and Heather. "Get inside." He pushed Blaine ahead of him and tried to shut the door. Before the latch caught a body slammed against the door forcing it open, and a wild-eyed Evans burst into the shop. Other men pounded at his heels.

Evans panted, "We'll fort up here."

The panic hadn't touched all the men for most of them carried their weapons. Haun slammed the door as the last one entered and turned a snarling face toward Evans. "You wouldn't listen, would you?"

"Shut up!" Evans screamed in fury. "Shut up!"

A bullet entered a crack between logs, and a man standing in the middle of the room uttered a broken groan and fell. The room was suddenly filled with angry bees with lethal stings.

"This is no fort," Haun said bitterly. "They got a million places to shoot through."

Heather's face was frozen with terror, and Blaine licked dry lips.

Emily said calmly, "I'm worried about them."

Haun nodded. "I'm fixing to do something about it." He opened a door to a small closet beside the forge. "I keep my old rags here." He pushed Heather inside and said, "Crouch down." He covered her with the rags. He looked at his work and said sorrowfully, "It's the best I can do."

He led Blaine to the bellows and said, "Slide under it, son. And you, sister, I got nothing left for you but a corner."

"Bless you," Emily said.

His smile was bitter. "For what? Nobody's out of this yet."

Terror held Heather in its iron clamp. She wanted to scream under its pressure, and she couldn't move her tongue. She heard yells of anger and pain, and the sounds of bullets never stopped. They made a hard thwock as they plowed into wood and a much softer, uglier sound as they entered flesh. Oh God, she prayed. Save them. Save them.

It lasted an eternity. Then above the din she heard Evans shout, "Every man for himself. We'll be slaughtered if we stay in here."

The door creaked on its hinges, and she heard the pound of running feet. The rifle fire increased in intensity, and she knew many of those men would never make it.

The firing faded to an occasional shot then stopped. The silence was as bad as the din. Her body ached from her cramped position, but she dared not move.

"Blaine," she whispered. "Aunt Emily." She feared to speak louder, and the silence mocked her.

She stiffened as she heard the sound of many feet coming through the door then the room was filled with loud voices and laughter. "I told you them Mormons were yellow," someone yelled. "Did you see them run?"

"Not all of them," a callous voice said.

"Hey," the first voice said. "Here's one hiding under the bellows."

Heather heard a small, scuffling noise and knew Blaine was being dragged from his hiding place.

"You let me alone," Blaine yelled. "I haven't done anything."

"Don't shoot him," the voice who had discovered him said. "He's only a boy."

"Nits grow up to be lice," the callous voice said.

Heather moaned deep in her throat at the sound of a shot. Her senses were slipping away, and she was sure she was going to faint.

Another voice saved her from fainting. "What have we got here?" She froze as the closet door was flung open. "Only old rags," the voice said in disgust. A rifle barrel was thrust into the rags, and it brushed her shoulder. "That's all," the voice said. The door was slammed with violence.

She bit her lip hard to keep from fainting. One moment she was clear-headed, and the next she was drifting. She had no idea how long she remained in the closet. Time was only an aching period of torment to body and spirit. She heard the heavy feet leave the building, and still she didn't move. Oh God, how could she be sure they had gone?

She heard other feet, and despair seized her. She had suffered too much; she could not remain here a moment longer.

A woman screamed, and others joined her. The wild sobbings pounded at her ears, but it was safe to come out. If the women had returned it was a sure sign that the raiders were gone.

She threw open the door and almost fell with the first step. She cried out at the agony of returning circulation to her stiffened legs and forced herself to take another step.

She looked about with dazed eyes. She saw the scene but for a moment she couldn't absorb it. Men lay everywhere on the floor, and women kneeled or sat beside them. Some cried silently, and others held dead faces to their bosoms, rocking back and forth as they wailed their despair. A few women still moved about the room looking for their men.

She didn't want to look toward the bellows but she had to. Blaine lay on his back, and his face was stamped with a final agony.

She screamed loud and piercingly, and it cut through all the grief in the room and turned faces toward her. Haun was just coming in the door, and he hurried to her. He glanced at Blaine then at the far corner of the room. He took her arm and pulled her toward the door. "Come on," he said gently. "It won't do you any good to stay here."

She followed him without protest. Her face was too frozen, her eyes too glazed. Haun kept glancing at her; he was unable to hide his concern for her. He wished she would cry and wail, anything but this trancelike sleep.

"He's dead, isn't he?" she whispered.

"Yes. And your aunt too." It had a brutal directness, but he hoped it would jar her into tears.

Her lips quivered, and her words were jerky and weak. "Why? He was only a boy."

"Because he was a Mormon," Haun said wearily. "They need no other reason. Those men were Gentiles dressed like Indians." His face twisted with an unequalled savagery. "God damn them all."

She whispered, "Blaine," and the tears started. She

was blind with them, and Haun took her into his arms. He patted her shoulder with a gnarled, hard hand and let her cry it out.

"Father wanted us to go with him," she said brokenly. "If we had listened to him—"

Haun said wearily, "If Evans had listened to him we could have been warned in time to slip away through the woods. And Evans didn't get a scratch." A wondering note crept into his voice. "I didn't either for that matter. When I ran out that door bullets sang all around me like mad bees. I guess I ran pretty good for an old man."

He noticed her crying was stopping, and that was good.

She raised her face. "So much grief and misery and I think only of my own. What can I do?"

He patted her shoulder in approval. "There's a lot to be done. They killed seventeen of us. Some more will die. They stole everything they could carry off. We need your help. We need—" He peered into her face. "Are you sure you're—"

She wiped her eyes. "I'm all right. Are you afraid I can't do it?"

She had seen some bad sights. She would see more. "Yes," he said helplessly.

"Show me what to do," she said, and her voice was firm.

People filtered back from the south woods, and every additional pair of hands was welcome. Heather helped tend the wounded, and she saw more men die.

She didn't break. Her face became a little more white and set, but she didn't break. She helped in the pitiful preparations of bodies for burial. She almost cried aloud in protest at the burial then she realized nothing else could be done. There were so many of them and so few people to take care of the work. The bodies were carried on a wide plank to a large, unfinished well and slid into it. Hay and straw were spread over them, then everything was covered with a thin layer of dirt. She broke as Blaine and Emily were carried to the well. She ran to them, and Haun let her have a few moments with them. Then he pulled her away saying, "It won't do any good."

He looked at the glitter in her eyes, at the white immobility of her face. This wasn't the same girl at all that he had seen earlier this morning.

Heather turned away before the dirt was shoveled into the well. "I've got to get to Far West." She had to reach her father. He was all she had left.

Haun said, "It isn't safe. You don't know who's out there."

She looked at him with such fixed intensity that it frightened him. She was going if she had to walk every step of the way.

He sighed and said, "It wasn't safe here either. I'll get you a horse."

Chapter Eighteen

Gilliam wasn't far wrong in his estimate of the men who would march on Far West. General Atchinson, with militiamen from Clay and Clinton Counties, marched from Liberty, and General Lucas brought up his division from the south. The two forces joined on the Log Creek road from Richmond at ten o'clock in the morning. It made an impressive force totaling eighteen hundred men.

General Lucas called together all officers and read them Governor Boggs' orders. It denounced the Mormons in inflammatory terms and said every one of them must be driven from the state or exterminated. It gave no protection to Mormon life or property, and Verl saw the gleam in men's eyes. If the orders were followed out every excess would be committed upon Far West.

General Atchinson stood and exclaimed angrily, "I will not be a party to such inhuman orders."

Lucas said coldly, "You are at liberty to leave, sir."

"I will." Atchinson looked at the assembled men as though seeking backers then stalked away.

Lucas looked pleased. It left him in sole command. He said crisply, "You have your orders. We will move on Far West tomorrow."

Brigadier General A. W. Doniphan walked away from the meeting with Verl. He wore a short beard on his jawline, and his hair was unruly. He had an easy way about him that men liked. Verl had been on a hunting trip with him two years before, and he had got to know the man well.

Doniphan's eyes had an angry glint. "Lucas could have softened those orders. He could have warned that he would stand for no looting or pillaging. The man wants it this way."

Verl said, "I didn't see anybody follow Atchinson." He had revised his estimate of Atchinson.

Doniphan gave him an odd look. "Were you thinking of doing so?"

"No." The answer was curt. One way or another Verl was going into Far West.

Doniphan nodded. "I didn't think so. I thought we would do no more than go into Far West and disarm and disband the Mormon regiment. This turns it into a nasty job, but it has to be done. Or the bloodshed will only go on."

A slight smile was on his face. "You seem to know more about the Mormons than any of us. You've been in their city, and you've fought them."

Verl didn't ask him how he knew. He supposed some of the men in his company had been talking. A wince crossed his face. "I didn't do very well in that fight. I picked a bad camp site."

Doniphan said slowly, "I'd say you did a magnificent job. You drove them off after being surprised and outnumbered." He clapped his hand on Verl's shoulder. "I'll see you."

Verl watched him walk away, then moved to rejoin his company.

He and Gilliam sat by a campfire and talked a long time that night. Gilliam said, "Shelby's company just got here. I wonder what took them so long. They left the same time we did. They sure act worked up over something."

Verl didn't give a damn about Shelby's company. All he wanted was for the man to stay out of his way.

Gilliam said gloomily, "It's going to be hell tomorrow. But maybe it's best this way. Maybe we'll get it over with once and for all."

"It won't be best for the women and children."

Gilliam glared at him. "What do you think is worrying me?"

Verl stared into the fire. Where was Heather? Had the Phelpses reached Far West safely? Or was there any safety any place for a Mormon? He had heard that on the way here some of the militia companies had burned every Mormon cabin and wantonly shot down livestock and destroyed other property. Most of these men were men of the soil. What had possessed them that they could callously shoot livestock? It must be a mad sickness that lay shallowly buried in men, and Lucas and Boggs' orders would strip off the thin veneer. Gilliam had stated it mildly when he said there would be hell tomorrow.

He didn't sleep very well that night. All around him he heard men talking excitedly far into the night as they discussed what would happen tomorrow. Shelby's company made the night hideous with their whooping, and Verl wondered how long Lucas would stand for it.

They went forward in the morning and camped at Goose Creek, a mile south of Far West. Lucas immediately sent out scouts, and Verl approved. He didn't like the man, but he could find nothing wrong with his ability as a soldier.

Part of his men were still mounted when three of the scouts came dashing back. Verl saw the excitement in their faces as they reported to Lucas.

Lucas' face glowed with a savage light as he listened. Then he turned and called for Doniphan.

Doniphan listened then nodded. He turned and came toward Verl. "Verl, the scouts report a large body of horsemen are trying to make Far West. Lucas thinks they can be cut off. I'd like to take your company with me."

Verl didn't belong to Doniphan's brigade, but he said, "Yes, sir." He ordered the company forward, and he saw their eyes gleam at the prospect of a fight.

Two hundred men rode out of the timber toward Far West. The scouts' report was correct. At least fifty men were riding hard toward the town from the northwest. They were much closer to it than Doniphan's force, and Verl saw they couldn't possibly cut them off. He wondered if the band was Norton and his Danites, and his eyes burned. But it would be a long chance that this particular bunch were the Danites, for Mormons all over the state would be trying to reach Far West. He doubted that Doniphan would go in now, and he tried to hide his disappointment.

His heart jumped as Doniphan moved forward

slowly. Doniphan was going in. He was amply backed. Lucas had had General Parks and a portion of Robert Wilson's mounted in reserve in relief of Doniphan if needed. Verl thought an all-out assault would carry the town.

Doniphan stopped within two hundred yards of Far West. The Mormons had thrown up a line of earthworks all about the town. A head-on attack against those breastworks could be a costly thing.

Doniphan sat there a long time studying the emplacements.

"Look, General," somebody shouted hoarsely.

Doniphan had already seen it. Mounted men rode through a gap in the fortifications. They fanned out on either side then wheeled into line. It was an awesome force of arms.

Doniphan called Verl to him. "How many, Verl?"

Verl remembered the force he had seen drilling in the town square. This looked to be about the same size. "I'd say seven or eight hundred men."

"I'd make it about the same," Doniphan said musingly. "Do you think that's all of them?"

"I'd say so, sir." It was only a guess, but Verl didn't think Far West could produce many more armed men.

Doniphan said, "Lucas will be relieved to hear it." He studied the general layout of the town; he had seen its defense and defenders. The information had to be carried back to Lucas and evaluated.

Doniphan swept his arm down toward the timber, and his force wheeled and rode away.

Verl heard the derisive yells from the massed Mormons. It grated on other nerves for he saw many a face turn and glare at them.

Verl hadn't been back at camp a half hour when he was called to Lucas' staff meeting. He felt stiff and awkward among all the higher rank.

Lucas nodded and said, "Sit down, Captain. I hear you've fought them already."

"Yes, sir."

"Wouldn't you say they are cowardly fighters?" Lucas asked eagerly.

Verl remembered how the Mormons had attacked across the river. "No, sir. I'd say they're about as tough as we could go up against."

Anger swept Lucas' face. It wasn't the answer he wanted at all. He said abruptly, "General Doniphan tells me you've been in Far West. Tell me about the town."

Verl sketched the way it lay in the dust before Lucas' feet, and Lucas watched with absorbed interest.

"If we carry the outer defenses what will we run into? More earthen works?"

Verl remembered the excavation for the temple. The Mormons had shown ability to accomplish tremendous work in a short time. But still there had to be a limit to what they could do in a given time. "I doubt it, sir. I don't think they've had enough time."

"Thank you, Captain," Lucas dismissed him. "You've been a help."

Verl walked back to the campfire and told Gilliam about it. He finished soberly, "I think it'll come in the morning, Sam. It's going to cost both sides."

A chilly wind whipped through the timber, and he added several more sticks to the fire. The Mormons wouldn't surprise Lucas. He had his scouts out and well-placed.

Gilliam crawled into his blankets and tucked them tightly about his neck. He said with wry humor, "Don't call me in the morning."

Verl sat there until the dropping temperature forced him to put more wood on the fire or crawl into his blankets. He decided on the blankets. He thought sleep would never come. He lay there and listened to the measured tread of the sentries about camp. Perhaps the sound had its mesmerizing effect for his eyes slowly closed.

He caught the tension in the camp the moment he awakened. Last night men had laughed and joked for the attack wasn't until tomorrow. Now tomorrow was here, and all the laughter was gone. When they talked it was in muted voices. Men polished rifles that were already gleaming or checked over their ammunition for the dozenth time.

Hoady came by as Verl was finishing tying his bedroll behind his saddle. He gave Verl a tight grin. "I hear those Mormon breastworks are going to be tough to take."

"Tough enough when there's somebody behind them shooting at you," Verl said.

Hoady started to say something when the stir of excitement spreading through the camp stopped him. It was strongest at the perimeter of the camp, and men jumped up and down trying to see what was going on.

Verl heard somebody shout, "It's a Mormon. They're bringing him in under a flag of truce."

The troops parted to give the rider and his two flanking attendants passage. Verl saw the man then. He carried a white handkerchief tied to a stick. His face was solemn, and he looked straight ahead.

"What's he want?" Hoady demanded.

"He hasn't told me a thing," Verl said soberly.

"Aw, you know what I mean."

Verl grinned. "I'd say we'll have to wait and find out."

The three men were escorted to General Lucas' tent. Verl saw Doniphan and other generals hurry there. Whatever the conference was, it didn't take long.

The Mormons came out of the tent, mounted, and rode back slowly.

"I wouldn't let them go," Verl heard a man say. "That'd be three less to shoot back at us."

Verl started to say hotly, he's carrying a flag of truce. But words wouldn't accomplish a thing. The man saw that flag.

Lucas came out of the tent followed by his staff. They talked for a few moments then moved back to their respective commands. The urgency seemed gone from their stride.

Doniphan saw Verl and beckoned to him. When Verl

joined him Doniphan asked in a low voice, "Do you know a Colonel Hinkle?"

Verl shook his head.

"He commands the Mormon regiment. He sent a messenger asking for a meeting with Lucas. Is it a trick?"

Verl gave it some thought. Because of his visit to Far West he was considered an expert on the Mormons. He thought ruefully, he knew as little about them as anybody here. But he wasn't going to say so. He wasn't going to destroy his prized seat at the inner councils.

"Maybe," he said cautiously. "Where's the meeting going to be?"

"On that high point of ground halfway between the town and our camp site."

The Mormons would be in view for a long way. Verl saw no possibility of an ambush. "I don't see what we can lose by meeting with him."

"My sentiments. The meeting's at two this afternoon. Be ready to attend it." He added as an afterthought, "It's not to be talked about."

"No, sir."

Verl walked back to where Hoady stood, and Hoady asked, "What was all that about?"

Verl shrugged. "They don't tell me a thing."

Hoady stared at him suspiciously. "You've gotten high and mighty since you've been mingling with the brass. You hoping for a promotion?"

Verl's grin had an infuriating quality. "I might be."

Hoady snorted and left him.

The hours dragged, and the troops grumbled about it. The high moment of tension was gone, and they complained about the delay. They'd grumble just as much if they were ordered forward now, Verl thought.

At one-thirty he fell in behind Lucas and his staff. Lucas was going to be early. It wouldn't take more than fifteen minutes to reach that high point of ground.

The horses stomped fretfully as they waited, and the tossing of their heads jingled bridle chains. Lucas sat like a man of stone, his face turned toward Far West.

The scene seemed peaceful enough except for that raw scar of breastworks before the town. And every now and then the watery sun glinted from a rifle barrel.

Doniphan said suddenly, "They're coming sir."

Six men rode out from the town, one man slightly in the lead. They came forward with a measured slowness, and it seemed it took them forever to reach the high point. The man in the lead stopped his horse and saluted Lucas. "General Lucas, sir? Colonel Hinkle commanding the Caldwell regiment."

Lucas returned the salute; his face was frosty. "What do you want, Colonel?"

Emotion twitched in Hinkle's face. He was a tall man with a lean, sunburned face. He felt his responsibility, for his shoulders seemed to sag under it.

"To discuss this affair, General. Isn't there some compromise, some other settlement of our difficulty without war?"

"None," Lucas said crisply.

Color washed Hinkle's face at Lucas' abruptness. "We could cost you dear if you attack."

"And it will cost you dearer if we do. I've got two thousand men in those woods, Colonel. If you force us to attack I promise you not a male Mormon will be left. And I make no promise concerning the women."

Hinkle wilted visibly. "And the alternative," he asked hoarsely.

Lucas pulled a folded paper from an inner pocket. He opened it and said, "These are the governor's orders. You are to give up Joseph Smith and the other leaders to be tried and punished for insurrection. All arms of every description are to be given up. The Mormons who took up arms will have their property appropriated to pay for all damages and the cost of the war. All those not held for trial will leave the state. They will receive protection from my troops until they are clear of Missouri."

Hinkle's face was bloodless, and his lips trembled. "My God, sir. You drive a hard bargain."

"You know the alternative," Lucas said coldly.

Hinkle looked at his folded hands on the saddle horn. They seemed to clasp each other tightly. "I must have time to confer with other people. I ask until morning."

"Until the morning," Lucas granted. "But I want Joseph Smith, Sidney Rigdon, Lyman Wight, Parley Pratt and George Robison to hold as hostages until I'm sure you'll meet the governor's terms. I will give you

189

an hour by sun in the evening to produce the hostages."

Hinkle shut his eyes tightly for a moment. When he opened them they were dull with the crushing weight of defeat.

"Agreed," he said.

"We march on Far West by an hour and a half by sun," Lucas warned. "I'd advise you to remember you can stop it by bringing the hostages."

Hinkle's head was erect as he saluted him, but his eyes were unseeing. He turned and rode slowly back toward the town.

Lucas' face held a wicked satisfaction. "They're crumbling. And I had rather hoped they wouldn't."

Doniphan dropped back beside Verl.

Verl asked, "Do you think he'll take it?"

Doniphan was silent. His eyes were on Hinkle making his slow way back to Far West.

"I think he will," he said finally. "His own reports have told him how many men we have. And he'll know of every piece of artillery that will be brought to bear on him. He hasn't even a choice to consider." His eyes were again on Hinkle. "You just saw a proud and sensitive man broken," he said almost absently.

Chapter Nineteen

Colonel Hinkle's face was wooden as he rode toward Far West. Only his eyes showed his inner sickness. He had six hundred men against two thousand—and worse, he had no cannon with which to hold the Gentiles off. The Gentiles had artillery. They could place cannon on the heights less than three hundred yards from town and pound it to pieces. They wouldn't even have to gamble their troops in an assault until the breastworks were leveled. The Mormons would fight. Particularly when they heard Lucas' terms. They would fight with determination and bravery, and either was a poor substitute for superior weapons.

His mind was filled with anguish as he ran over the possibilities. If he reported his meeting with Lucas as it had occurred he would see the town bathed in blood—Mormon blood. Smith and the other leaders would never agree to the terms. He glanced back at his staff officers. They had remained well back in his meeting with Lucas, and he was certain none of them had heard the talk. He could twist what had happened in any direction, and none of them could say it wasn't so.

His experience and conscience grappled, and his conscience was stronger forcing him into a terrible decision. He would be flayed by his people, but God knew he wasn't wrong. It was far better to save lives than to throw them away in a useless cause.

He rode through the gap in the breastworks and dismissed the officers. Men cheered him as he passed them, and he heard one of them yell, "I'll bet you told them, Colonel."

He kept his face stiffly forward as he proceeded to Joseph Smith's house.

Smith came out of the door to meet him. He was a

man small in stature, and his eyes were harried. His black beard and hair were unkempt, and Hinkle knew that Smith had spent worried hours ever since the trouble broke. He wondered what Smith would do if the man were in his own position.

"What happened, Colonel?" Smith asked tensely.

Hinkle shook his head. "Nothing much. I didn't have enough authority to complete the talk. General Lucas wants the leaders of the church to talk to him. He is willing to listen to a compromise or a truce." He named the men Lucas wanted.

Smith asked eagerly, "Then it can be settled peacefully?"

Hinkle nodded. "The meeting is to be this evening."

The tenseness in Smith's face was fading. "I'll get the others. We must not weaken our stand with them. They must agree to some of our conditions."

He walked down the street with a rapid stride.

Hinkle watched him go, and there was a stinging behind his eyes. God help him now. It was done.

Only Lucas' officers guessed what might happen. Lucas went ahead with normal battle preparations. The order had been issued to the troops that they would march on Far West by an hour and a half by sun. General Parks' mounted brigade was to form on the right of the division as flankers, and if required was to pass entirely around the town and to attack it from the rear on the report of cannon. The cannon was to be the signal for a general attack. General Graham's brigade was on the extreme left, and Doniphan's and Wilson's brigades were to form in line of battle on foot to the south of town. The artillery company and its cannon was to proceed ahead of Doniphan and Wilson and to occupy the height within three hundred yards of town.

Lucas kept an eye on the sun as he went over his final preparations. He had thought the hostages would be here by now. He wasn't sure if he was glad or sorry. He hated the Mormons, and he wanted to crush them. But despite the most careful planning a man could never know exactly how a battle would go. If the Mormons resisted he wouldn't lead as many men back as he was leading forward. He thought viciously, for every pint of blood the Mormons spilled he would spill gallons.

He looked at the sun again. It wouldn't hurt to move a little early. If the Mormons were weakening a display of force might be the shove they needed.

He gave final instructions to his staff, and they scurried away to their commands.

It took a little time to put an army in motion, but they made an impressive sight as they came out of the woods. Lucas looked up and down the long line and was satisfied.

The line moved relentlessly forward, a hungry wave ready to engulf the town ahead. Lucas felt the tension mounting within him. It was only a matter of minutes now.

He peered ahead in the gathering gloom and sighed.

A small party was moving toward him under a flag of truce. The tenseness spilled out of him. He knew it was the hostages. The Mormons had capitulated.

Hinkle rode forward to meet him.

"Are all of the hostages here?" Lucas asked.

"All of them," Hinkle answered in a dead voice.

Lucas turned his head and barked an order. Troops hurried forward and formed a strong guard about the Mormons. Smith turned an agonized face toward Hinkle as he realized what was happening.

"Traitor," he screamed.

Rough hands seized the hostages and hurried them back to camp. Joseph Smith kept looking back and screaming "Traitor" at Hinkle.

Lucas stared at Hinkle. "We will enter Far West in the morning to take your surrender."

Hinkle nodded numbly. His face looked as though it was carved out of white marble.

Lucas rubbed his hands together after Hinkle had left. "I'll take their town without firing a shot. Who said there was bravery among the Mormons?"

Verl rode back to camp with Doniphan. "Damn him," he said savagely. "He should be grateful he'll have an easy time, and instead he's boasting about it."

Doniphan's face was stern. "You're talking about a superior officer, Captain."

Verl said stubbornly, "I don't give a damn."

A grin twitched at Doniphan's lips, then he laughed. His face sobered. "Those people are going to suffer. And Lucas thinks only of the glory it'll bring him.

He's wrong about there being no bravery among them. It took a brave man to do what Hinkle did." He sighed and said, "Lord, I'm tired."

Verl felt the same way. He supposed it was because he had been stretched tight for so long. Now the letdown was more exhausting than physical work.

Upon impulse he said, "Have supper with us, General. My men killed some squirrels this afternoon. I have an excellent cook."

"Accepted. I'll join you as soon as I see my men settled."

Hoady was skinning a brace of squirrel when Verl found him.

"I thought I counted five squirrel," Verl said.

"Clarkson took the others. He shot them. They were his."

"Will that be enough for three of us?"

"Who's coming?" Hoady asked suspiciously.

"Doniphan. I just asked him."

Hoady finished skinning the squirrels. He held them up, and they didn't look very big. "I'll make some gravy and stretch them." His eyes turned serious. "I wish Doniphan was in command of this." He shook his head. "That Lucas is too much of a strutting man to please me."

Verl could agree with that. Lucas had already shown his harshness toward the Mormons. And Verl doubted the man would have any inclination to protect their individual safety tomorrow. If the Phelpses had reached Far West he hoped he could find them quickly. He wanted to make Heather's safety his personal responsibility.

Doniphan appeared as the meat was browning in a skillet. He sniffed and said, "That smells good." He sat down and watched the cooking with absorbed interest.

Hoady stirred some flour into the drippings and added water. He sliced bread and said, "General, this bread is as hard as a rock. Maybe the gravy will soften it."

He filled a tin plate and handed it to Doniphan. He watched anxiously as Doniphan took the first bite.

Doniphan said solemnly, "I never expect to taste better."

Hoady beamed with pleasure.

They ate in silence, and Doniphan took a piece of bread and sopped up the last of the gravy. He smiled and said, "If my wife could see me now." He filled a pipe and offered the tobacco sack to Verl.

Verl shook his head. "What's going to happen to them tomorrow?"

Doniphan knew who he meant for his face sobered. "They'll be expelled from the state. I doubt if they're allowed to leave with more than the clothes on their backs."

"Hell," Hoady said indignantly. "They've worked hard for what they've got. It doesn't seem right."

Doniphan said mockingly, "It has to be right. They believe differently than we do. Whatever we do to them is right."

Verl stared into the fire. "Will it ever change?"

"I doubt it," Doniphan said wearily. He started to add something when a trooper came up to the fire.

The man said, "Sir, General Lucas wants to see you immediately."

Doniphan's eyes sharpened. "Tell the general I'll be there right away." He waited until the trooper left and said, "Come along, Verl. This might be interesting."

Lucas was pacing before his tent when they arrived. He gave Verl a harsh glance, but his words were for Doniphan.

"General, the staff officers just finished a meeting. It was decided in the interest of keeping a permanent peace that Joseph Smith and the other prisoners are to be executed. You are to take them into the public square of Far West and shoot them at nine o'clock in the morning."

Verl sucked in his breath. He expected a roar of disapproval from Doniphan, but Doniphan's voice was calm.

"Why wasn't I notified of the meeting?"

Lucas lifted his hands and let them fall. "We looked for you. We couldn't find you."

Doniphan said bitingly, "You found me easy enough a moment ago."

Lucas colored. "Are you questioning me?"

"Yes," Doniphan snapped, "And I'll tell you what I think of your orders. It's cold-blooded murder. I will not obey. My brigade shall march to Liberty at eight o'clock in the morning. If you execute those men I will hold you responsible before an earthly tribunal, so help me God."

"General," Lucas roared.

Doniphan's voice softened to an ominous note. "And I don't think even the governor would approve when he hears that you captured those hostages by trickery. And don't forget, sir, I have a witness."

Lucas wilted. He tried to stare Doniphan down and couldn't. He pointed to a tent a few yards away. It was strongly guarded. A light in the tent silhouetted kneeling men against the canvas wall, and Verl knew the Mormons were praying.

"General," Lucas muttered, "I never intended for you to carry out that order. I wanted Smith to hear what could happen to him if he doesn't advise surrender."

Verl sickened at Lucas' duplicity. He doubted that the prisoners could hear the conversation.

"I'm glad to hear that," Doniphan said dryly. "I'm still pulling my men out in the morning."

He turned and walked away, and Verl followed him.

Verl said, "You can't leave." Doniphan was one of the few men here who might show compassion.

"I've got to. Did you believe what he said at the last?"

"No."

"Neither did I. My leaving might keep some kind of a check on him. He'll be wondering whose ear I have." He started away then came back. "Verl, all those people in Far West don't need punishment. It's going to be harsh enough as it is."

Verl nodded. "I'll remember."

' were the mildest of the abuse hurled at him.
...ord had leaked to them of Hinkle's part—or
...sed. But either way they crucified him with
...d looks.

...uld see only the man's profile, but he was
...e were tears on his cheek.

...ected Lucas to dismiss his troops, but he still
...m in formation. Lucas' orders came down
...command, and Verl felt a sick disgust. The
...s to march all through town. This was Lucas'
...glory, and he was squeezing it to extremes.

...arch was an endless one to Verl. Not a street
...sed, and while nobody was on the streets he
...ly a curtain flutter at windows as a spectator
...back. The Mormons didn't need this final
...y to know they were beaten.

...ondered which house Heather was in. He kept
...he would see her face at a window, but that
...e too much to ask for.

...dismissed the troops after the march. Many of
...mons still stood in the square under guard, and
...ndered how long Lucas would hold them there.
...nan had given the troops no warning against
...and pillaging, and the tacit omission gave full
...to any excess.

...saw a dozen bottles come into view a few
...ts after Lucas disappeared. Far West was in for
...of hell.

...as free to take up his own search for Mace
.... He prowled the town looking for him. He

Doniphan pressed his shoulder. "Come up into my country. I owe you a hunting trip."

"I'll do that, sir."

Verl watched Doniphan until he was out of sight. He dreaded the morrow. If the Mormons knew what was in store for them they would dread a lot of following days.

Chapter Twenty

Lucas' army was lined up in parade front as it moved forward. Only Doniphan's brigade was missing.

The sky was overcast, and a biting wind blew out of the north. If moisture fell Verl thought it could go either way—snow or rain.

The troops still weren't aware of what had happened. They knew the Mormon leaders had been taken captive, but they still expected a fight from the town.

Verl had told Gilliam the situation, and Gilliam looked up and down the long line. "Most of them are strung tight," he commented. "Pluck them and they'd twang." He sighed and finished, "I'm getting too old for this. I'm glad you told me."

Verl nodded. It was still a tense scene to him. The earthen-works ahead were silent, and the army was steadily cutting down the distance to the town. With Doniphan gone he no longer knew what came out of higher council. Had there been a change? He worried about that. He had expected some kind of display from the Mormons denoting surrender, and he had seen none.

They were within range of the breastworks, and Lucas rode ahead of his troops. Verl drew confidence from that. Lucas wouldn't do that if he expected gunfire.

They were within fifty yards, and still he saw no movement. He couldn't keep the frightening thought out of his mind—they were riding into an ambush. At any moment they would face a withering blast of fire. But the church leaders were still under guard back at the camp. Would the Mormons jeopardize them? He wished he knew.

All along the earthen line the head logs of the breastworks suddenly tumbled outwards, and a half-dozen white flags went up. Verl didn't realize he sighed.

They rode into Far West, and the Mormon companies were moving as a regiment into the public square. Hinkle formed them into a hollow square, and for a moment the two forces confronted each other.

Verl looked at wooden faces. Only the eyes showed any emotion. There was hating in those eyes, but a beaten hating. He didn't see a single woman. He imagined they were behind locked doors. This was the start of the fearful hours for them.

Hinkle rode forward and saluted Lucas. Slowly he unbuckled his sword belt and drawing his pistol he handed both weapons to Lucas.

Verl felt the tension slipping away from the men behind him. It rose in the air like a great sigh as they realized what was happening. The Mormons were surrendering without a fight.

Then yelling broke out, wave[...] hugged one another in their re[...] without firing a shot.

Lucas waited patiently until t[...] all armed men here?"

Hinkle was so beset with e[...] scarcely speak. "Six hundred m[...]

"You will deposit your arms," [...]

Mormon company after comp[...] and laid down their arms in the [...] It was a motley collection of [...] hunting rifles, shotguns and a fe[...] swords were crude and homema[...] bered the corn knives Norton's m[...] few pistols and wondered if all [...] turned in. A pistol was an easy we[...]

He watched each company as [...] Their faces changed as they put d[...] hating still remained, but it had ch[...] hopeless thing. He didn't see [...] watched for him. Still in that many [...] missed him.

Lucas detailed one company t[...] weapons and another to guard the [...]

He looked at Hinkle and said col[...] missed, Colonel."

Hinkle saluted for the last time. [...] looked close to the breaking po[...] through the loose formation of the [...] manded, and cries rose all aroun[...]

Betrayer[...] Maybe [...] they gue[...] words a[...]

Verl c[...] sure the[...]

He ex[...] held the[...] through [...] army w[...] hour of [...]

That [...] was mi[...] saw ma[...] jerked [...] indignit[...]

He w[...] hoping [...] would [...]

Luca[...] the Mo[...]

Verl w[...]

The [...] looting[...] consen[...]

Verl [...] mome[...] a nigh[...]

He [...] Norto[...]

knocked on doors and at most of them received no answer. He visited all the public places and asked questions. The questions weren't profitable either. Most of the Mormons looked at him with stony faces. A few muttered, "I never heard of him." They were lying, but he couldn't force an admission out of them. By nightfall he was beginning to doubt that Norton was in town. It was very possible that the Danites hadn't come in for the defense of Far West.

He crossed the public square again, and it was empty. Lucas had moved the prisoners somewhere, and Verl asked a passing trooper about it.

"He sent them back to our camp under guard, Captain. I heard he's going to select more prisoners to go with the original ones he wanted. He's marching them to Independence for trial. I guess he wants a big display when he gets there."

Verl said, "Probably," and moved on.

Three troopers came down the street toward him, and they were staggering drunk. One of them bumped into Verl, and he suspected it had been deliberate.

He shoved the man back and said sharply, "Watch where you're going."

The man crouched and snarled at Verl. He was spoiling for trouble, and he had manufactured his chance for it.

The other two grabbed him before he could spring. "Hey," one of them said, "that's one of our captains. Sorry, Captain," he apologized. "Hamp's been celebrating a little too much."

The belligerence was momentarily knocked out of Hamp. "Man's got a right to celebrate," he mumbled.

"If you keep it within bounds," Verl snapped. "You men had better report back to your companies."

Two of them gave him bland grins. "Why sure, Captain. Anything you say, Captain."

They staggered by him, and he watched them until they were out of sight. Too many troopers were in this same condition tonight. Those three were looking for Mormons. It would be an unlucky Mormon who fell into their hands.

Verl moved on. Even though he had covered the town he would search it again—and then again. He turned a corner and saw Gilliam just ahead of him.

"Sam," he called. He hurried his pace and caught up with Gilliam. "What's an old man doing wandering around in a strange town at night?"

"I feel older than that," Gilliam sighed. "I've been all over town, Verl. I haven't seen him."

Verl knew who he meant, and he said, "It's my business, Sam. Stay out of it."

"Hell, Verl. I wasn't going to do anything if I found him except to come and get you."

Verl's hand rested briefly on Gilliam's shoulder. It was apology and an expression of gratitude. "It's still my business, Sam. I'm beginning to believe he's not in town. Unless he's hiding."

"He could've slipped out. Maybe before we got here."

Verl had considered that. It would have had to have been before they got here, for Lucas had thrown a heavy guard around town with instructions to shoot any Mormon who tried to slip through. A man would have to move like a puff of smoke to escape the notice of those guards.

He said, "Maybe."

Gilliam peered at him. "You're going to keep looking?"

"I've got to."

Gilliam nodded his understanding. "Let me know if you run into anything you can't handle."

"I will." Verl watched Gilliam move away. He wished Gilliam wasn't so concerned. Somehow it was wrong after what had happened with Elly.

He began his patient plodding again. His reason and aching leg muscles told him it was useless. In the darkness one man would look much like another. Norton could pass across the street from him, and Verl wouldn't know it.

He saw a great deal of drunkenness and evidence of plundering. He stopped one militiaman wearing a lady's shirt-waist over his outer coat. She had to be a lady of ample girth.

"Where did you get that?" he demanded.

The man teetered back and forth, and the fan of his breath was whisky-laden. "Why Captain, the lady gave it to me."

"Take it off."

The man obeyed, but his face was sullen. "Don't you think we deserve a little fun after what we been through?"

Verl eyed him coldly. The man hadn't really been through anything. He wondered where the man had stolen the garment, and he knew he'd never find out.

He said, "Not that kind of fun."

He looked back after a dozen yards. The man was pulling the shirtwaist over his head again. Verl put down the impulse to turn back. That was probably just a minor bit of plundering compared to what was happening all over town. And he couldn't police it all by himself.

The wind grew colder and except for the campfires all other lights in town were extinguished. Verl felt the teeth of the wind. He was a damned fool to be tramping around on this useless quest when he could be lying by a fire wrapped in his blankets.

He had decided to abandon the search—at least for tonight—when he saw a furtive figure slip out of a house ahead of him. Verl melted into deeper shadow and stopped. The man stood motionless for what seemed an eternity then struck out swiftly in the opposite direction.

A hard throb of excitement pounded in Verl. He might not have paid any attention to the man except for the garment he wore. It was long and white, and it stood out distinctly in the darkness. Norton had worn an overcoat made of white blanket material in that fight on the river.

Verl debated briefly. If he ran after Norton the pound of his feet would alarm the man. He had a good half block advantage, and he knew the town better than

Verl did. Besides Norton could run into any house, and its occupants would hide him.

He saw Norton turn at the corner and made his decision. If he went the opposite way around the block he might run squarely into the man. And he might lose him. That was the chance he would have to take.

He whirled and ran down the block. He turned to his left at the corner and ran another block. He didn't slow for that left turn. His breathing had a tinge of fire when he reached the end of the block. He stopped and heard the sound of approaching footsteps. He didn't dare look to see who it was. The footsteps were too close.

He drew his pistol and forced his breathing shallow and slow unless even that small sound gave him away. The footsteps sounded right on top of him when he stepped out into the open.

The light wasn't good. At first all he could see was the white blur of the overcoat. He heard the man's startled grunt and saw the animal-wariness seize the figure.

His eyes conditioned to the light, and he could make out the hated figure. "Norton," he said coldly. "I told you I'd be back in your country."

Norton recognized him at the same time, and the suck of his breath had a harried sound.

"You bastard," Verl snarled.

Some sound broke past Norton's lips, part grunt and part fear. He fought the buttons of his overcoat, and Verl waited. Norton wouldn't have dared carry a weapon openly. He would have it concealed deep on his person, and Verl wanted him to think he was going to reach it.

He saw Norton sweep aside the tail of his overcoat, and he fired. The shot slammed Norton back a broken step, and his head flung high. His breathing had a whistling sound, but he still fought to dig his hand into his inner pocket.

Verl shot him again, and Norton bent forward. He made sobbing groans as he tried to stay on his feet. He had a desperate, futile vitality for he still sought to get his gun clear.

Verl shot him a third time. Norton's head flung clear back this time then snapped forward. His knees buckled, and he sank to the walk. He hung there an instant then pitched forward. His hand was still in his pocket.

Verl stared at him dispassionately. He hadn't given Norton much chance. He hadn't intended to.

He heard startled cries coming from several directions. Militiamen would he here in a few moments, and there would be questions. Verl had no fear of punishment. He had killed a Mormon trying to escape, and that would satisfy anybody. But there was no need to face any kind of investigation.

The cries were nearer. He looked down at Norton for a moment, then melted away. He had thought he would feel an elation when he killed the man. He felt nothing but the dogged weariness that pulled at him.

Chapter Twenty-One

The touch of a cold drizzle on his face awakened Verl in the morning. It must have been drizzling for some time for his blankets were beaded with moisture. He smelled coffee and turned his head. Gilliam and Hoady had a fire going and coffee boiling. Both sight and smell were never more welcome.

Verl stood and shivered. It was going to take a lot of basking by the fire to drive the cold misery out of his bones. He moved to the fire, and Hoady said, "If it keeps at it it could turn to snow."

Verl nodded. A good, heavy snow was all they needed to make things completely miserable.

Hoady poured a cup of coffee and handed it to him. "Did you hear the news?"

A muscle in Verl's cheek twitched. Hoady was probably talking about Norton. It was neither important nor news.

"General Clark is coming in with two thousand men to take over the town. Lucas is leaving with his prisoners. He wants to get them back to Independence." Hoady shook his head. "I sure hope we don't draw the job of guarding them. I don't want to ride clear to Independence."

Verl didn't either. He was not popular with Lucas. Lucas might pick his company as a form of punishment.

Gilliam hadn't said anything. His eyes were still on Verl's face. They were sharp eyes. They picked at a man's brain.

"You found him." He made it a positive statement. Verl nodded.

"I thought so when I heard those shots last night."

Hoady gave them a puzzled look. "What are you talking about? I didn't hear any shots."

Verl said, "You could sleep through cannon fire."

Hoady grinned. "That's because I've got a clear conscience." The grin faded. Something more important was on Hoady's mind, and he went to it. "Man, I sure hope we don't have to go to Independence. I want to get home."

Home! The word had a hollow ring. Verl's future looked vague and disconnected. If he could find Heather he might be able to put it back together.

Gilliam's eyes were studying him again. He hoped Gilliam couldn't read his thoughts of the moment.

Lucas picked his guard, and Verl's company wasn't among it. Shelby and his Indians were, and Verl guessed at what Lucas had in mind. Shelby's company would add color to the display when Lucas marched into Independence.

Over a hundred Mormons were under guard. There weren't that many leaders, Verl thought, as he watched them being marched out of town. The great majority of them were just little men acting under orders. They were torn from their families and would walk many a weary mile before they reached Independence. But they would make Lucas' victory impressive.

"What do we do now?" Hoady asked.

"Wait for Clark," Verl answered. Clark was to take over all duties when he arrived.

"I hope he gets here today," Hoady grumbled. "Waiting in an unfriendly town isn't very pleasant."

It wasn't pleasant for the Mormons either, Verl thought. More of them were on the streets this morning. It was odd how much they looked alike—a pair of dead eyes in wooden faces.

Hoady watched a couple of them across the street. "You know I kinda feel sorry for them. Even though they started it."

Did they? Verl thought wearily. That was a question that would be argued many times. The Mormons would have one version and the Gentiles another. And maybe it would never be satisfactorily settled.

He moved off, and Hoady called after him, "Where are you going?"

"Just looking around," Verl answered without turning his head. His tone carried no invitation for Hoady to join him.

He began a new search. If Heather was in Far West he would find her. Asking questions was useless. He had learned that in his search for Norton. He wished he could make a house to house hunt. He would know quickly whether or not she was here. He supposed he could, but he dreaded going that far. It would be an invasion of what little privacy the Mormons had left.

All he could really do was to watch the shops. Surely she would need necessities. More of the

Mormon women were in evidence. They hurried by him with downcast eyes. Each time he saw a slender figure his hope returned. A few seconds later and it was gone.

He discontinued his search at nightfall. She wouldn't be out on the streets at night.

He heard quarrelsome voices around him as he tried to go to sleep. Men were impatient for Clark to arrive. They wanted to go home.

Would Heather be different when he found her? She has to be, he thought, and tried to put conviction into it. She had to see the futility of all this. She would listen to him now. He was still arguing with himself when he went to sleep.

He awakened in the morning and stared at heavy clouds on the northern horizon. A snowflake touched his face. A heavy snow would add to the Mormon misery. None of them had been allowed outside town, and many of them must be getting low on firewood. Some of the restrictions would have to be lifted to allow men to go out and cut wood.

He resumed his patient search. He was even emboldened enough to ask a Mormon woman if she knew Heather Phelps. She backed away from him with wide-eyed fright then turned and ran. He sighed wearily. He would get no help from that source.

The weather couldn't make up its mind what it wanted to do. It would snow hard for a few moments then stop. The clouds would thin and weaken, and just when one thought they were parting to let the sun through they packed together, and it started snowing again. By noon an inch of snow was on the ground.

Outside of town the white blanket was unsullied except for the tracks of the wild animals. Inside the snow was churned to dirty slush.

General John Clark of Howard County arrived with two thousand men shortly after noon. Verl knew nothing about the man, but he hoped he had more pity than Lucas. Surely, those stringent restrictions would be lifted and the Mormons be allowed to leave the town and forage for food and wood. Verl suspected both commodities were running low for the Mormons.

If anything Clark tightened the restrictions. No Mormon was allowed to leave town regardless of the errand. At the end of two days Verl couldn't see smoke coming from a single Mormon chimney. The temperature was dropping into the teens at night. That was brutally cold weather for an unheated house. He thought he could see the pinch of hunger in Mormon faces, and every child he saw had a runny nose.

"What's he trying to do?" Gilliam asked. "Drive them to rebellion?"

Verl knew how Gilliam felt. This was getting to be a hard thing to watch. He said in a low voice, "He knows they can't fight us with just their bare hands. I think he was sent here to put the final pressure on them."

He pointed to a foraging party just entering town. A skinned carcass of a young beef was draped over a pack horse. "But we're doing all right," he said savagely. "We're stripping the country. If Clark doesn't stop his men there won't be any food left for the Mormons."

Gilliam nodded grimly. The militia was foraging liberally upon the corn still in the fields and on the flocks and herds. There had been some wanton burning of buildings for he had seen several black smoke plumes in the sky. "Watching this makes you feel real proud," he said.

"We're not going to watch it much longer," Verl said. "If Clark doesn't release us we're going anyway." He had abandoned his search for Heather. He was convinced she wasn't in Far West. The thought that he'd probably never see her again numbed him more than the cold.

"I'll see him again this afternoon. We'll leave tonight—with or without his consent."

He couldn't get in to see Clark. A staff officer turned him away saying, "The general is busy with his speech he's going to give to the Mormons in an hour." The man laughed. "He's got them softened up enough. They'll listen to him."

Verl questioned him, but the man would say no more. "Listen to his speech. You'll find out."

The Mormons were assembled in the temple square when Clark made his appearance. He sat his horse and looked coldly at the assembled throng. He held a sheet of paper in his hand, and he read from it.

"You have lost your leaders and your arms. Now you must sign over all your property to defray the expense of the war. When that is done you will be allowed to go into your fields to obtain food. In a few weeks you must leave the state forever. If you don't your families will be destroyed."

He lifted his head; there was a sorrowful look on his face. "It hurts me to see people in such a fix. You will never see your leaders again. I wish I could deliver you from the awful chains of superstition and liberate you from the fetters of fanaticism. But that rests solely with you. I advise you to scatter and never again organize with bishops."

Verl and Gilliam were standing at the rear of the crowd. Verl had been right with his guess. Clark had been sent as the final, crushing boot.

"The hypocrite," he said fiercely. "He steals from them then tells them how sorry he is."

"What will they do?" Gilliam asked.

"They'll sign over their property. What else can they do? They've got hungry women and children."

The Mormons were breaking up into little segments to discuss Clark's speech. Verl didn't see a spark of resistance in a single, haggard face. This new blow had completely flattened them. Yes they'd sign—for the chance to find food and wood.

His shame was a churning sickness in his stomach. Thieves, he thought. That's all we are.

He said, "Have the company ready to move in an hour." He could take no more accusation from the dull eyes in this town.

He moved away from Gilliam. Though it was use-

215

less he wanted to make one more turn around the town. Heather wasn't here. But this was a final bit of self-torture he must indulge himself in.

He left the temple square and walked down a side street. He tensed as a woman came out of a house a half block ahead. Her back was toward him, but she moved with the same beautiful grace he so remembered. He would not let himself be deluded again, he would follow no more will-of-the-wisps. Despite his assertions he found himself quickening his pace. He wished he could see the color of her hair, but she wore a scarf tied over it.

"Heather." The call burst impulsively from his lips.

The woman stopped and turned, and dear God, it was she.

His heart sang a paean of joy, and its reflection shone from his face. He ran toward her, his hands outstretched.

She shrank back from him as though his touch was contamination, and the gesture dealt a clubbing blow to his joy.

He dropped his hands. "I've been looking for you for days." This wasn't the same girl who was lodged in his head. Her cheeks were haggard, and her eyes listless. Even the fullness of her mouth seemed to have thinned.

He reproached himself for the criticism. She had gone through some harsh privations.

"I've been afraid to go out until today," she said.

Her eyes looked at him as though he stood a great

distance away, and he had the feeling he must shout to reach her.

"If you knew how I've been worrying about you—"

"Have you," she said bitterly, and the accusation he knew so well was in her voice.

He said appalled, "My God, Heather. You don't think I—"

"You are with them." Her face asked what more proof was needed.

He wished he could touch her. It might break down this terrible wall between them. "I had to come, Heather. Because it was my duty. But I did everything I could to ease things for your people."

"Duty," she almost screamed at him. Her face was ugly with its loathing. "Was it your duty to steal everything my people have? Was it your duty to kill Blaine?" The loathing in her face broke, and she looked like a little, whimpering girl.

He was truly shocked. "Blaine dead? How?"

Her eyes searched his face, and there was an agony of entreaty in them. Briefly, she described what had happened at the mill. "They tried to disguise themselves as Indians. But they were white men. They were Gentiles."

For an instant he thought the wall might be breaking. That was Shelby's Indians. He'd find the man responsible and reckon with him later.

"But I didn't do it, Heather. Don't you see—"

The entreaty was gone from her eyes, and the wall was as intact as it ever was. "Your people did," she said dully. To her it was the same thing.

Once there had been a sweet, warm moment between them. Now there was only resentment.

He asked, "What will you do now, Heather?"

"Our people are talking about going to Illinois. We hope to find a friendlier land there."

He wanted to tell her she wouldn't. That as long as they set themselves apart from other people those people would tear at that aloofness trying to batter it down. It had happened in Independence, in Caldwell County, and it would happen again in Illinois. But he couldn't explain it so that she could understand.

He said, "I promise you one thing, Heather. I'll find the man who killed Blaine."

The weary resignation was back in her face. "It doesn't matter now."

"It matters to me. Blaine was my friend."

There was nothing more to say, and still he clung to this meeting. The memories of the dead dreams were crying inside him.

"Goodbye, Heather." They were the hardest two words he had ever said in his life.

She turned away without answering him.

He walked rapidly down the street and never looked back.

Chapter Twenty-Two

Verl entered Britton's house without knocking. Britton was sitting in a chair, his feet outstretched to the warmth of the pot-bellied stove. He jumped at the sound of Verl's entrance then said angrily, "Dammit, Verl. You might give a man a little warning."

Verl's eyes swept the room. Britton had acquired several new items. Two shotguns and a hunting rifle stood in the far corner, and Verl had never seen them before. He had never seen that mounted rack of deer horns or the china lamp. He wondered how many items Britton had managed to carry away.

His silence made Britton uneasy. "We beat you home by several days, Verl. General Lucas put on quite a parade in Independence."

Verl could imagine. His expression didn't change.

"I guess we're rid of them for good, huh, Verl?" Britton's eyes kept shifting. He didn't like that look on Verl's face.

Verl said softly, "Been collecting a few things, Britton?"

Britton shrugged. "I had a few extra dollars. I got me some bargains."

"You're a God damned liar."

Britton blinked, and his face went defensive. He put bluster into his words, but they still sounded hollow. "You got no right to come into a man's house and say something like that."

Verl moved to the chair and looked down at Britton. "You took those things from Haun's Mill."

A nerve jumped in Britton's cheek. "All right. Suppose I did. It wasn't any worse than anybody did in Far West."

"No worse," Verl murmured.

"I'm getting mad at you, Verl, coming in here and jumping me. A man's got a right—"

"You really believe in rights, Britton?"

"You're damned right I do," Britton shouted.

"Who killed the boy?" Verl fired the question suddenly.

Britton's face went slack with surprise, and an uneasy flicker appeared in his eyes. "I don't know what you're talking about," he said sullenly. He knew all right.

Verl's hand fastened on his shoulder. It could have been Britton himself. He jerked him to his feet, and Britton yelled in outrage.

"Who was it?"

Britton's face was contorted with passion. "You get out of my house, Verl Wakeman. You get out right—"

Verl hit the man in the mouth. The blow knocked him down and he landed awkwardly. He turned dazed eyes up at Verl. He was bleeding at the mouth.

He gasped, "Have you gone crazy?"

"Tell me who killed the boy. I can stand here and beat on you the rest of the day." He saw the stubborn set of Britton's jaw. "All right, Britton. We'll take the hard road."

220

He pulled Britton to his feet and hit him again. He made sure his blow wasn't too heavy or landed in a spot that would knock Britton out.

Britton went down again. His face showed both anger and fear. He put a hand to his bleeding face then looked at the red smears on it.

"By God, I'm going to have you arrested. You wait and see."

Verl seized him again. "You keep this up, and you won't be able to talk." His face and voice showed no passion. He might have been discussing the weather.

He jerked Britton to his feet, and Britton flailed at the arm holding him. He was a little man, and his strength made no impression on that arm.

Verl hit him on the forehead. Britton went over backwards and landed on the chair. His weight splintered it. Now only fear showed in his face.

"I tell you I don't know."

"I think you do."

Britton flashed a glance at the guns standing in the corner.

"If you crawl toward them I'll kick you to pieces." Verl stood over him showing no pity. "You can stop this any time you want to." He reached down for him, and Britton tried to crawl from the outstretched hand. But he crawled in the opposite direction from the guns.

Verl pulled him to his feet. Britton's legs didn't want to support him, and Verl had to hold him erect.

"Damn you, Verl," Britton whimpered.

Verl drew back his fist.

"Don't hit me again," Britton squalled.

"Who was it?"

Britton's resistance collapsed. "He'll kill me," he wailed.

"There won't be much left of you to kill."

Britton squeezed his eyes shut, and tears rolled down his cheek. "It was Shelby," he said in a shaking voice. "I yelled at him he was only a boy. But Shelby said nits grow up to be lice."

Maybe Britton had tried to save Blaine. It wasn't important. Verl let go of Britton, and he fell. Hs turned and walked to the door.

"Verl," Britton screamed.

Verl looked at him. The hating blazed in Britton's eyes.

"I hope he kills you."

"He's going to get his chance." Verl closed the door behind him.

He mounted and rode off without looking back. He had no fear that Britton might grab up one of the guns. Britton's spirit never reached very deep. He was probably still on the floor sobbing out his rage.

Verl rode into Gallatin and stopped before Gilliam's office. Gilliam sat behind his desk. His face looked grayer.

"Have you seen Shelby?"

Gilliam considered it. "He was in town earlier. He might still be here. Why?"

"I'm going to kill him."

Gilliam's eyes didn't even jump. "Do you want to talk about it?"

"He killed a twelve-year-old boy. Without reason."

"The Phelps boy?"

"Yes."

Gilliam shook his head. "He seemed like a nice kid. You're sure it was Shelby?"

"I'm sure. I told you because I don't want you trying to stop me."

"Why I'll be tied up all afternoon with paperwork."

Verl nodded and started for the door.

Gilliam's voice stopped him. "Verl, be careful."

Verl nodded again.

He went down the street. Except for the burned-out houses the town looked normal. He supposed the rebuilding of them would be put off until spring when the weather was better. Most of the people had moved back, and they were trying to pick up the dropped threads of their lives. He hadn't seen Elly yet, and he hoped he wouldn't run into her. He couldn't say exactly why, but he had a dread of seeing her.

He stopped in at the blacksmith shop, and Hoady said, "Man, the work that's piled up. If you've got something busted you're going to have to wait."

"No work, Hoady. I'm looking for Shelby. Have you seen him?"

Hoady gave him a probing glance, but his curiosity wasn't aroused enough to push further. "He was in about fifteen minutes ago. He's probably still in town."

Verl said, "Thanks," and walked out onto the street. He stopped methodically in each of the town's business places leaving the saloon to the last. At each place his search was negative. The saloon was the last building on this side of the block, and he moved to it. He stopped before its door and tucked the skirts of his mackinaw behind the pistol butt. He pulled the gun halfway from its holster and let it drop back. It slid easily.

He stepped inside, and the big, pot-bellied stove in the far corner was a cherry red. The room was too hot.

Shelby stood at the end of the bar. Laughter was on his face as he raised a glass to his lips. Five men, counting Markey the bartender, were in the room.

Verl stopped just inside the door and planted his feet wide. His hands hung down by his side, and there was blazing hatred in his eyes.

"Shelby."

Heads swung toward him. Every man saw the hard passion in his face, they saw the tucked-back coattails. They saw the spring-steel tenseness of his posture and recognized it for what it was.

Shelby's face went pinched. He set his glass down carefully and let his hand rest within an inch of a bottle. "Verl," he said. The word came out dry and brittle.

"You son of a bitch." Verl's voice was flat. "You killed that boy at Haun's Mill."

The blood rushed from Shelby's face, and sweat popped out suddenly on his forehead. "I don't know what you're talking about." The jerkiness of his words said he was lying.

"Then I'm going to make a mistake. I'm going to kill you anyway."

Shelby's lips quivered, and his face was wet. "I'm unarmed."

"So was the boy."

A drunk picked that moment to enter the saloon. He staggered against the door throwing it hard against Verl's hip. It knocked him off balance. Shelby's hand closed on the bottle, and he threw it at Verl. Verl tried to regain his balance and duck the bottle at the same time. He had to take his eyes off Shelby, and Shelby bolted into the back room.

The drunk insisted upon making apologies, and Verl had to throw him out of the way. When Verl looked up Shelby was gone. He heard the slam of a door and pounded for it. He threw it open, and the door at the opposite side of the room was just closing. Fear had pumped speed into Shelby's feet.

Verl ran through the storeroom and jerked the outer door open. He stepped outside and caught a glimpse of Shelby turning the corner of the building. He grunted and picked up speed. He whipped around the corner and saw Shelby crouched a dozen yards before him. Shelby had used his brief time well: his gun was out and aimed at Verl, and Verl knew he couldn't beat Shelby to the shot.

Something slammed into his left shoulder with brutal force, spinning him half around. He felt only a shocking numbness that somehow weakened his knees. He tried to lock them in place, and they insisted on buckling. He took a broken step then plunged on his face. Only fragments of thoughts entered his mind, and he couldn't sort them and place them in proper order.

He heard the pound of running feet, and he had to think about it before he realized what was happening. He raised his head, and Shelby was running. He thought wonderingly about it. Shelby could have finished him, but he was running in the opposite direction.

He spat dust out of his mouth and tried to sit up. He wanted to follow Shelby. God, how he wanted to follow, but his muscles wouldn't respond.

He cursed those slack muscles. Pain was beginning to push the numbness out of his body. It took only furtive nibbles at first then it opened its ravenous jaws and devoured him. He thought it would empty his stomach, and he gagged against the sour sickness that filled his throat. But he discovered something. Some of his muscles could move. They had moved the hand that covered his mouth.

He tried again, and he could sit up. The pain locked his teeth together, and he had to wait until its fiery grip loosened. He got his feet under him and pushed off the ground. He had to plant his legs wide to keep upright, and the earth tilted and spun. His head hung low while he waited for the spell of nausea to pass. He could feel something warm and sticky flowing down his skin. He looked at his mackinaw, and the blood was beginning to soak the left front of it.

He gripped the pistol butt with an intensity that made his knuckles stand out. He was too late to get

Shelby—it had taken him an eternity to get off the ground—but he had to try.

He went toward the street, and in the short distance to it he had to lean against the building wall twice for support.

He was bleeding profusely, and it was sapping his strength. It made him light-headed and put dipping, weaving colored lights before his eyes.

As he reached the street he thought he heard the drum of hoofs. It was getting so hard to think clearly now. Why was somebody riding a horse that hard?

He saw a massive blur moving rapidly down the street toward him. He peered at it, and a name flashed into his mind. Shelby! It had the effect of a stiff wind, it broomed his mind free of the fog. Shelby could have escaped on foot, but instead he had run for his horse. It had taken him time to reach and mount it, and why he was racing out this end of town instead of in the opposite direction Verl would never know.

He had only a brief respite from the black fog that insisted upon rolling back. He cursed the unsteadiness of his hand as he tried to hold the gun steady upon the man on horseback. The muzzle wobbled in uneven circles, and he groaned in anguish of spirit. The darkness was rushing at him, and he was sure he wouldn't get more than this one shot. He pulled the trigger, and from far off he thought he heard a man scream. Then he was inside the mouth of the black tunnel and sliding rapidly down its tilted floor.

He opened his eyes, and the light in the room hurt them. He squeezed them tight. Surely just the little movement of opening his eyes couldn't have started all that pain in his chest.

He heard someone call, "Elly. He's coming to. He opened his eyes." He heard the light patter of footsteps, and a soft voice said anxiously, "Verl?"

He opened his eyes, and Elly was bending over him. Her face was drawn with worry. He stared at her a long moment. It was odd, but he had never noticed how truly beautiful her eyes were.

Gilliam stood on the other side of the bed, and his face had the same concerned cast.

"Shelby?" Verl asked. He was surprised at the weakness of his voice. That was only a whisper.

"You picked him right out of the saddle. He's dead."

"Ah." The word contained an immense amount of satisfaction. "I made a fool mistake, Sam. I made—"

Elly placed her fingers over his lips. "You mustn't talk now."

He had to talk. He wanted to know a lot of things, and he had to explain as many more. "He hit me hard?"

Gilliam said almost cheerfully, "Just missed a lung. You bled like a stuck pig. When we picked you up I thought you were dead."

Elly's eyes blazed at her grandfather. "Sam," she said in rebuke.

Gilliam grinned. "He's all right now. When he opened his eyes I knew he was going to make it. He's too ornery to die."

Verl's eyes swept the room. He had to think about it a moment before he realized where he was. He was in Elly's bedroom again. His shoulder was freshly bandaged, and he'd bet she'd done that.

He grinned feebly. "I seem to make a habit of winding up here."

For some reason that brought a blush to her face. "You mustn't talk." She tried to say it severely.

He had never really looked at her before. Her face had softened, and an inner radiance was shining through. What had ever made him think she was a plain woman?

Gilliam was tiptoeing out of the room, and Verl couldn't understand that. He didn't want to waste time thinking about it not with her standing so near.

He said, "Elly, Shelby killed her brother. He was just a twelve-year-old kid."

She said in an oddly flat voice. "She's very beautiful."

Some of the radiance seemed to be fading from her face, and he wanted desperately to call it back. He thought about her statement. Heather hadn't been so beautiful the last time he saw her, and that was the way he would remember her.

"I guess she was," he said. The cause of that fading radiance hit him suddenly. He could bring it back. He knew he could.

"Elly, a man's got to be a fool at some time in his

life. He gets off his road and kind of flounders along. I guess I'm lucky. I got back on the road."

Wonder of wonders! The radiance was coming back into her face. But he couldn't understand the sheen of tears in her eyes.

"Elly," he said plaintively. "Can't you help me? I'm trying to say I love you."

"Oh, Verl." She was crying openly now, but it wasn't a sad crying. She tried to steady her face and voice. "No more talking tonight."

But he had to talk. He had to talk about her, about their future together. "Can I talk in the morning then?"

She leaned down and kissed him lightly on the lips. "You can talk tomorrow." It was a big promise. It included all the tomorrows ahead of them.